TO THE BONE

Ken Lindsey

DEDICATION

This book, along with everything I have ever done right, is dedicated to my kids. My big girl, my princess, my baby girl, and my baby boy—nothing would be worth it without you kids there to cheer me on.

Also, to the girl who speaks for the trees: Thank you for always being honest. Everything I write is better because you read it first.

CONTENTS

PROLOGUE

The girl ran through the deserted park faster than she had ever run in her life. The cold night air pressed against her tear-soaked cheeks like sandpaper, forcing her to wipe her face with her sleeves as she went. He followed behind her somewhere, but she no longer heard his pounding feet. A stitch of pain raged in her chest, and another in her side, as her muscles cramped in protest.

She slid under the old jungle gym, hoping that the orange glow from the streetlights around the playground might keep him from coming after her. She swallowed and gasped and gulped in the air selfishly, trying to refill her aching lungs and give her body a chance to recover. Wood chips dug into her skin wherever it touched the ground, but she refused to move a muscle.

She flinched when a breeze spun the merry-go-round at the opposite end of the playground, making it creek. Her heart beat like a drum line, crashing within her chest and throbbing deep in her ears. Keeping as still as she could, the girl looked up and down the street. Nothing. Yet. Maybe he had given up the chase.

A stick cracked somewhere off to her left, making her gasp and jump, slamming her head against the underside of the jungle gym. She bit her lip as stars blurred her vision. The girl wanted to yell or scream or cuss, but knew deep inside that silence was her only chance to stay hidden. She gingerly ran two fingers along the sore spot on the top of her head and the fingers came away warm and wet with blood.

Dread. It was a word she didn't think she had ever used, but the only one that seemed to describe her feelings in that moment.

Then a pair of headlights turned onto the road which outlined the west edge of the park. The engine sounded soft, and the lights were bright. In those lights, she saw her salvation. She would run to the street, wave down the car, and get the driver to give her a ride to the police station. Even if he hid with her there in the park, close to the playground, she saw no way he could beat her to the fence if she ran with everything she had.

The car came closer. She took in a deep, steadying breath through her nose and scooted forward using her elbows and knees. Carefully, she inched her way out from under the jungle gym. Once out, she climbed to her feet and dusted the wood chips from her knees. She flinched and looked around in a panic as the debris rained softly to the ground. No movement in the park. No sound.

The car pulled to only a hundred yards away. It was now or never.

She counted herself down silently. Three.

Two.

One!

Before her first step landed, something above her snatched a handful of her hair and she screamed, all thoughts of running lost. With no time to react, he yanked her up off her feet and pulled the girl over the bright red railing of the jungle gym, slamming her to the hard-plastic grating next to the swinging bridge. More pain. More stars.

He pinned her body with one knee on her sternum and the other on her stomach and clapped his hand down over her mouth. "Ssshhhh, Jennifer," he whispered, bringing his nose only an inch from hers. His breath swelled hot and wet on her face. His eyes shone wide and hungry in the pallid light of the oncoming car, with only a sliver of green bordering his overly dilated pupils.

She took in shallow breaths through her nose. He held her still and silent until the car passed. It felt like an eternity.

Once the car drove safely beyond the park, he gave her a grin that made her skin prickle. A second without his hand over her mouth, and then something rough and wet took its place. The cloying smell drove everything else away, and with her next breath the world turned gray.

1 MORNING HAZE

The song from my phone's ringer filtered into my head while I slept. My ex-wife danced on my grave, then spat on it. The tang of the previous night's stale fries and whiskey rolled around on my tongue as I woke up and a brand-new hangover scratched back and forth in my skull with every movement.

The music stopped as I got out of bed. I ignored the phone and grabbed the last cigarette in the crumpled pack on my nightstand. Wasn't my brand, but since I found myself all alone on my big Queen mattress, I called *finders keepers* and lit the bitch up. The first drag burned, but covered the flavor of the night before, so it didn't bother me.

My phone rang again. As I snatched it up from the nightstand, I realized the music was wrong. Early jazz, which meant I had gotten an email. They were always the same: BeachBunny49 wants your hard on right now, or BarelyLegalSteven is brewing a load to your liking. Stupid spam. Get drunk and visit one little transvestite porn site... Never again.

The phone light flicked on and I took eight tries to get the digital slider thing to move over. The message bar showed a missed call from Yvette, which may explain the dreams I had. I remembered the night before and decided I may have gotten low enough to drunk dial my ex.

I cleared the missed call notification and moved on to the email. The heading looked vague enough to be porn, "Saw your ad," but the sender's name didn't have a bunch of numbers after it, so it might have been legit. I opened it up.

-Hello,

I'm not sure why I'm doing this. I need help. My daughter has been missing for almost a week, she ran away... That's what the cops say. I want to find her. I don't think she would go like this, but I need to know for sure. If she hates me or doesn't want to be here, that's fine. She's old enough to take care of herself. But if it's something else... I think it is.

Please help me. I don't have a lot of money, but I'll beg borrow and steal to find out the truth. If you are willing to help, please call me.

Thank you,
Rachel
775-555-1505

They're always runaways. Parents suck and teenagers suck and eventually someone needs to get away. It would be an easy fare, so with a little techno-magic I don't understand, I pushed the number and saved it to my contacts list. I'd call her after I got coffee and a greasy breakfast to clear the cobwebs.

I still had residual wood, so my morning piss came hard and I had to clean up the side of the toilet when I finished. After I flushed, I looked in the mirror. It wasn't pretty; someone left a swollen hickey on my neck, which I didn't remember getting, and my lip had some dried blood covering a split that still tasted of pennies. That might mean a fight, or it could mean good sex, but I had no idea which. I ran my fingers over the stubble on my chin. It wasn't too long yet, but I hated the gray I saw sprouting up. I gave myself a quick shave.

In the kitchen, I ground coffee beans and boiled water and threw them both into the French press. As I started thinking about making breakfast, my phone rang again. This time a heavy metal guy screamed about how a girl lit his clothes on fire. My ex-wife. I slid the answer bar to take the call.

"Thanks for calling Gavin's pimpin' house of pimpery. Can we slap something up for you today?"

"You are such an asshole." Yep, that's her, my blushing bride of yesteryear.

"Good morning to you, too, Yvette."

"It's bad enough that you get drunk and call me begging for sex every other damn night, why in thirty blasted hells would you call Mike?"

Shit. Last night must have been a riot. If only I could remember it. "I don't know, Yvette. Maybe I got nostalgic and wanted to bend his ear for a minute."

"Goddamn it, Gavin! I didn't get a second of sleep last night because he kept playing your voicemail, over and over. *'Yvette, did you let him do that to you? You never let me do that, you said never ever.'* You described our honeymoon to him!"

I didn't try to bite back the laugh. I wanted to listen to that voicemail as much as I had ever wanted anything, but if I asked I'd be in even deeper trouble.

"You're an asshole!" It was her special squealing holler, which meant we were heading for a meltdown.

"I'm sorry, hun. I don't remember anything from last night. If it makes you feel better, someone punched me in the face." I lied. "Do you want me to call him and apologize?"

"Fuck off, Gavin."

"Love you too."

After she hung up, I looked down at my fingers. My last cigarette in the world burned down to the filter and my heart broke a little. The universe had decided to make me leave the apartment today. Damn it. I hated leaving home, especially to buy cigarettes. Nevada isn't too bad as far as smoker rights, but in Reno, there's always a twelve-year-old at the counter who will give you a look when you ask for a pack. A look that says, *'You're as bad as Hitler for smoking that cigarette.'*

I pushed the plunger down in my French press and watched as the red water turned brown, then black. The scent sent an invigorating tingle down my back; I love coffee more than anything when I wake up. Not as much as I love whiskey at night, but that's apples and oranges. After rummaging through the cupboard, I found my Superman travel mug and filled it. The first sip went down hot and delicious, and it helped to part the morning haze.

I needed smokes, and I knew I should call the email girl back. Smokes first. I kicked through the laundry on my bedroom floor until I found last night's pants. My wallet was still there, and it even had a little cash in it. That's nice, perhaps the morning wouldn't be a total crapshoot. I shoved the wallet into my pocket and put the pants on. How dirty could they be?

After grudge-humping my Jeep through morning traffic for half an hour, I bought my cigarettes at a convenience store and walked to the coffee shop next door. I would be able to get more coffee, check out a few barista girls, and make my call there.***

One week before

Every breath she took hurt. She fought it as long as she could, hoping to stop breathing. Hoping that she would stop altogether.

She knew he wouldn't let it end until he finished with her, but a fleck of hope arrived hours before. The hope that the end was near, and he would let her go. He had someone new strapped down in the other bed. Another "*lover*" for him to spend his time with. With any luck, that meant that he planned to end her pain, let her die.

"Good morning, my darlings," he said as he flicked the light switch, illuminating the room with the pale-yellow glow of the bare bulb that hung overhead. The light caused her to flinch, suck in air too fast. A thousand tiny needles stabbed into her chest at once.

She strained against the strap that held her head down, trying to watch as he came into the room, following the same routine he had since she first arrived. He opened the closet next to the steel door. Took out a clear plastic apron and a pair of bright yellow dish washing gloves and put them on. He hummed an old battle hymn she only ever heard in the movies her dad watched when she was a little girl. Then he walked to her bed, wearing his usual smile.

"And how are we this morning, Denise?"

"Wonderful now," her voice sounded shallow, and the words came out slowly. "I missed you while you were gone." She learned the answer by her third day with him. You had to be polite if you wanted to eat. Nothing else changed. The knives still came, and the needles, and all the other things he used to both destroy her body and keep her alive.

"I'm glad you said that," he said as he leaned over and kissed her on the forehead. His breath reeked of mint. She remembered her first weeks with him; his breath had been minty then too. But that was so long ago that she had almost forgotten about it. Now it was minty again, and some black void inside her roared with jealousy. The mint was there because of the new girl.

"You smell nice," she whispered as he made his way to the sink where the knives were waiting.

"Thank you, *lover*. I figured that since this is our last day together, I should be extra fresh for you." She couldn't move her head to see what he was doing, but the water ran and the knives clinked against the metal bottom of the sink.

"What do you mean?"

"Well, Denise, our time together has been amazing. You've been a generous and fulfilling *lover*, and I will never forget you. However, you have nothing left to give and I need to move on without you."

For the briefest second, Denise imagined home and her mom and her friends. Then she remembered where she was, and what he did to her. Another deep breath, uncontrollable pain. The thought of death was even sweeter than her silly thoughts of home.

She didn't reply, and she had no way to wipe away the tears that were rolling down her cheeks. He came closer now, still smiling, and ran his thumb beneath her right eye. Something heavy slumped on the bed next to her.

"I want to introduce you to our new family member before you go though, Denise. I think you'll remember her. She's asleep still, so you won't be able to catch up, but I thought it might be nice for you to see a familiar face."

His arm slid under her neck while his other arm went beneath her hips and he lifted her from the bed as easily as he might move a baby from a crib. She struggled to not look at the remains of what had once been her body. Denise remembered running, pedaling a bike. She tried to stop remembering.

He carried her to the side of the other bed, the one that remained empty since her first day, all those months ago. He angled her body, and then her head, until she saw the form lying there, still as if she were sleeping.

It took a moment, but she realized that she recognized the girl in the bed. Her hair had grown longer, and she may have lost weight, but there was no mistaking her best friend.

Her chest burned and ached as the first sob escaped. "No. Please no."

He turned her away and started back toward her bed. "You wouldn't want me to be alone, would you, after you're gone?"

"Pleeeease..."

He laid her back on the bed with care, and she convulsed against the sheets as she cried.

"Don't ruin this, Denise." His voice changed, became darker. "I don't have time to argue with you. Our first meal needs to be prepared before she wakes up. It's important to make a good first impression, like I did with you."

Denise kept sobbing. She thought she might throw up, and she couldn't form words any longer. She looked on as he picked up the heavy thing from next to her. He moved it from the side of the bed, up to the head. He smiled again as he showed her the carpenter's hammer. It sounded heavy when set down next to her, but it looked like nothing in his hand, just a small piece of wood with a smaller hunk of metal at the end.

"We're going to have my favorite tonight, like you and I did on your first night at home. I only get it once in great while, and I've been looking forward to it for a long time."

As he lifted the hammer above her head, she remembered that first meal vividly. It had been tasty after two days with no food. After they ate, he told her that brains were considered a delicacy in many parts of the world.

She barely felt the hammer as it smashed through her temple.

2 COFFEE TIME

When I got up to the counter to get my coffee, a
thirty-something jock-itch with a manager's badge
met me with a terrifying grin. "What can we brew for
you today?"

"Black coffee, in a bucket. Biggest and darkest
you can give me."

"Sounds good, would you like a bagel or a pastry
with that?"

"No. How much?"

"Biggest, darkest coffee is a dollar even."

I threw a buck down and gave the girls in the
back a cursory glance. Cute. Next time.

Found a table by the window up front and took a
seat. After a few minutes, the jock-itch called my
order. I walked back to the counter and grabbed
my joe. When I turned around, someone new sat at
my table. Someone I did not want to see. Oh well,
too late.

"Hey there, partner," said Hank as I sat
down. He used the word loosely. Business had been

down a few months back, and he loaned me
cash. Just a thousand or ten, but somehow, he
thought that made us partners. "I've been trying to
get hold of you. I got another job for you to do."

It would be following his wife again. He cheated
as easily as the rest of us breathe, and had done so
even when we were in high school together, so he
assumed she had to be as well. Five or six times now,
he sent me out to follow her around and find out
where she went and who she went there with. It's the
same every time. She was a poor kid who married
into money, and she's not dumb enough to lose it all
to get her rocks off once or twice. But I owed him,
and we settled by lowering my bill. I didn't have
much choice.

"I'm not sure, Hank. There's something else
coming up today, a missing person gig. The kind that
helps me pay the bills so I don't need to borrow
money from you."

"That's good to hear, pal. Really, it's nice to
know business is good. But you, you're a smart guy
who can handle more than one iron in the fire,
right? It'll be a night or two, no biggie."

"Sure. But this time you take a thousand off my
tab and let me come to the set for your next movie."

"A thousand? That's reaching. And I can't have
you jerking off in the background while my actors are
trying to do a scene." "*Actors*," that was a joke. "Fine,
five hundred, and I won't jerk off. I can control
myself. I'm just curious, I wanna see how the magic
happens. And I've always wondered what
a fluffer does."

"Now that's more reasonable," replied Hank with
a sly smile. "Okay, buddy, I better take off. We're

shooting a couple things this week, and I need to take the Ford to the shop again. Every single time I park downtown, the thing gets vandalized."

"Shitty."

"Shitty's right. Too many scumbags out there." Hank stood, his gut hanging halfway across the table, and I shook his hand. "Tell me when you want to come by the set."

"When do you want me to tail the old lady?"

"She's doing something tonight; said she's going to a spinning class at eight. Whatever that is. If you could hang at about seven-thirty, that would probably work."

"All right."

"I've got a good feeling about tonight. I think this is the time you get something."

"That's not supposed to be a good thing, Crystal's your wife."

"You know what I mean."

Once Hank exited the building, I dumped the bucket of coffee into my empty travel mug, flashed a quick smile at the lady barista who had taken over at the counter, and walked out. I had a hope she would watch as I went out, but didn't look back to check. Rejection wouldn't do anything to make the morning better.

Outside, there were a few of those wrought-iron chairs and tables, with ash trays on them. I took a seat and lit up a cigarette. It was only Tuesday morning, so the streets of Reno were barren, just the way I liked them. The cigarette was good, and the coffee burned strong and rich down my throat. I felt better, almost ready to fake a smile, so I pulled my phone out of my pocket. I brought up the contact list, scrolled down to Rachel, and hit the green button.

It didn't ring. Instead, a lady robot came on and introduced a shitty indie band that played keyboards and harmonicas and a steel guitar. Before she answered the phone, I prayed I had the wrong number.

"Hello?" Her voice came through soft and a little scratchy, sultry even.

"Rachel?"

"Who's calling. please?"

"My name is Gavin English. I'm calling about an email I received this morning."

"Oh."

"Is this Rachel?"

"Are you the private detective, the one from Craigslist?"

"Yes, ma'am."

She paused, perhaps a moment of regret. "I don't want to ask for help. I want to believe she's mad and she ran away and she's somewhere safe. I just don't."

"Well, I'm sure I can do a little work to help ease your mind. At least find out for sure where she is even if you decide you want to let her be."

Silence again, "Yeah. All right. How do we do it?"

"Well, Rachel, when you have the time you should come down to my office. I need some recent pictures of... I'm sorry, what's your daughter's name?"

"Jennifer."

"Okay, yeah. I need pics of Jennifer, her social security number, bank info if she has any, and a list of friends who I can talk to."

"She doesn't have a bank account, she's sixteen."

"All right, but I need the rest."

"Yeah. Okay. Where's your office?"

I always hate this part. Nobody wants to take you seriously when your office is in a real "strip" mall. "Take 95 to Keystone and turn left. I'm on the left-hand side, right next to the big 'XXX' sign."

Another hesitation. "You're next to the strip club?"

"Yes, ma'am, prime real-estate for my line of work." It wasn't the truth, but I couldn't just say I'm too broke for anything else.

"Because a lot of strippers go missing over there, or because you're a perv?"

"You never know," I replied.

"You're not making this easier for me. I need someone I can trust, this is important."

"I get it, Rachel, I'm sorry. Just trying to lighten the mood."

She growled and hesitated for almost a full minute, then "Okay. I'll be there in about an hour."

"I'll be waiting."

As I stuffed the phone back into my pocket, I caught a whiff of my shirt. I still smelled like the night before and I looked like a bar hopper, not a private detective. This called for a quick shower and a fresh button-down and a pair of slacks. I needed to hurry if I wanted to beat her to the office.

Finishing the last of my coffee, I smashed another half-smoked butt into the plastic ashtray on the table. I ran to the parking lot next door, found the Jeep where I had left it, and jumped back onto the road.

3 MEET AND GREET

I hadn't been to the office in a few days, so when I got there I opened the window over my desk and turned on the air conditioner. It wasn't exactly hot, but definitely musty and smelled like old smoke. Nothing a little manufactured fresh air couldn't fix.

I showered in record time, so I had some leeway before she should arrive. I straightened up my desk, emptied the old ashtray, and picked up a loose Jameson bottle and other litter off the floor. I made sure there were two clean glasses and fresh ice on the table by the door; you can never guess when a client might need a stiff drink. Once the room aired out, I sprayed my ninety-nine-cent air freshener, and hid the can.

Before I knew it, the door buzzer rang out, and a woman walked in.

When you talk to a woman who has a sixteen-year-old daughter, you get a certain picture in your mind. Crow's feet. Minivan. Mom butt.

This woman did not meet the description. She had thick brown hair, with a tight cut and highlights that looked natural. She had curves, but only enough to make you take notice. Her legs were smooth and coiled all the way from the floor to her ass. She had a tattoo on her calf of something with wicked-looking wings that traveled past her knee and up into the hemline of her thigh-high skirt. Other than a look of panic in her eyes, she appeared cool and in charge.

Love at first sight. Whatever that means.

"Rachel?" I asked as I took my fedora off. Some people tell me the hat's too much for my line of work. I tell those people to eat dick. I like the hat.

She nodded and stepped forward. I walked out from behind my desk and shook her hand. Soft skin, cool but dry.

"As I said on the phone, I'm Gavin English. I would say it's a pleasure to meet you, but under the circumstances..."

"It's fine, Mr. English," she replied. "Everyone keeps telling me I'm crazy, but she's my daughter. I'm sure they're right, but I need more than assumptions." She had an accent I hadn't noticed over the phone.

"Of course." I used one of the few gentlemanly moves I had and gestured to the chair in front of my desk. "Please, have a seat. You can call me Gavin."

"Okay," she answered as she sat. "I brought the stuff you asked for," she said, laying a stack of papers on my desk.

I sat across from her. "Where are you from?"

"What do you mean?"

"Is that an East Coast accent? New England by chance?"

"Boston. I can't believe you can hear it, I haven't been there since I was little."

"Jennifer never lived there? No one on the East Coast she might be hiding out with?"

"No, she's lived in Nevada her entire life."

I flipped through the papers. I had a list of phone numbers and names, a birth certificate, a school picture and a few others that were more candid, and even medical records. This woman wanted answers. Some parents just want to be sure they won't get in trouble for the stupid things their kids might do on their own, but not her. Her voice trembled and her eyes shown with genuine worry for her daughter.

"I hate to ask, but where's her father?"

"Prison."

"For?"

"Why does it matter?"

"It might not, but I can't be sure if you don't tell me."

She looked away from me for the first time. At the wall. At the desk. Her daughter's picture. "You need to understand, Mr. English. He was a good guy, but a gambler. He got drunk one night and held up a gas station."

"I see. Probably not important, but it's good to know. Are you still married?" It wasn't pertinent to the case, but a little extra information never hurt. Especially where beautiful women were concerned.

"We never were."

"All right." I fought back a smile and turned my attention to the papers. "I'm guessing that some people on your contact list are under eighteen?"

"Yeah, I'll talk to their parents if I need to."

"That'd help out a lot. Tell them I might be calling. Try not to freak them out."

She looked confused for a moment. When it passed, "Yeah, all right."

"Are all of her boyfriends on there, like *all* of them?"

"Yeah," she replied. "I'm not an idiot."

"I have to check, Rachel. Some parents don't want the truth about what their kids are doing while they're growing up. You want a drink?"

"No." She crossed her legs and leaned back in the chair. Back in control. "Now I guess we talk about your fee."

I got up and poured myself a drink. Her looks could kill, but I had bills. I needed to be fair, but to get info on Jenny's social life and find out if anyone on her list had a record, I was going to pay. She turned in the seat and looked at me as I took a drink. I swallowed too hard, coughed.

"I'm gonna need a thousand for the week."

She turned away. "Yeah, maybe I will have a drink."

"Rocks?"

"Please."

I poured her two fingers over a couple of ice cubes and bought myself some time walking back to my seat. "There are costs involved. I'm not a cop anymore. I have to pay folks to pull reports and files."

"It's fine," she lied. We both knew it. She downed the glass without flinching and I stared as she licked the moisture from her lips. "I can give you five hundred now, so you can start. I'll pay the rest at the end of the week."

How could I say "no" after she went through all the trouble of wearing her shortest skirt and brightest lipstick? I must have sounded hard up over the phone.

"I don't normally do that, but I want to help you out."

"Thank you, Gavin."

Three fucking hells, the eyes she gave me then... Could she blush like that on command? As my heart got softer, the rest of me stiffened up.

"No problem."

She took the cash out of her bra. Her bra! Five hundred, right there. She didn't even look at it before handing it over. Jesus, was I so transparent that she pegged me over the phone?

I laughed. The corner of her mouth lifted in what might have been a smirk. I had no chance and that was just fine by me.

4 THE RAIL

I threw Rachel's paperwork into a manila envelope and locked the door. Morning was long gone by the time she left and I only had a few hours before I needed to get on Crystal's tail. Goddamn Hank. I tossed the envelope in through the window of the Jeep and lit a smoke to help me think.

David Reeves was the only detective who would run files for me. A long time ago, in a galaxy far, far away, David and I were partners. We got along well, and he even testified on my behalf once, before I left the department.

Now, though, I owed him money. Oh well. I would have to pay him. Then he could run Jennifer's social, see if she popped up in any schools or even on a credit check. I would give him the names on the list too, see if we had any violent records or anything else that might ring a bell.

Once I finished my cigarette, I flicked it under the Jeep and climbed in behind the wheel. I tried to think of anything but those legs, those lips, that ass. Reaching out to David was the first thing on my list. I needed to get him the info and go home for a drink and a nap. It was destined to be another long night.

I pulled out my phone and dialed David's number.

Two rings, "What now?"

"David! I was just thinking about you and remembered that I owed you a little money."

"Is that so?" his tone lightened up a bit. "Does that mean you're going to pay me for once?"

"That's the plan, buddy."

"All right then, want to meet up for a drink, your treat?"

"Sure thing. I've got a little something to toss your way anyhow."

"Of course you do," another tone change. Why are people always eager to be in a shitty mood? "No more promises. If you want me to run your files, you pay first."

"No problem. Why don't you meet me at The Rail at 6pm?"

"Fine, but if you're passed out under another stripper, I'm going to take my money from your wallet and leave you there."

"Ha-ha, no worries, I have to work tonight. It's a two-drink limit for me."

"Sure," then he hung up.

I drove home, had a drink, and slept until a quarter after five. I have no idea what I dreamed about, but I woke up thinking of Rachel. Another glass of Jameson. Made a quick call to remind David to meet me and got his voicemail. Got back in my jeans and threw on a hoodie for the long night. At the gas station, I grabbed another pack of smokes and broke a few twenties down to singles.

The traffic was shit. I arrived at a quarter after six and the bouncer charged me twenty dollars to get in. Arguing the price crossed my mind, but the guy wore a frown uglier than Hitler's mustache, and he had to have had at least a hundred pounds on me. I paid with a smile and an Andrew Jackson and walked past as quickly as possible. When I found David at the bar, he had two drinks in front of him.

"You owe her thirty dollars," he said, pointing to the brunette behind the bar.

"No problem," I said as I sat down and picked up the glass closest to me.

"And you have my one-fifty, right?"

I took a sip as I imagined the little cash I had disappearing before it even had a chance to warm my wallet. "Sure do, plus another hundred for the new stuff."

"That's good," he replied, smiling at me for the first time in quite a while. I knew David liked me, but he was good at pretending otherwise. He polished off his drink in one gulp and waved the bartender over.

"You still owe for that one," she yelled over the stage music. She had several piercings in one ear, one in her eyebrow, and two in her nose. I wondered what she would be like in the sack.

"My friend is paying," David hollered back.

She looked at me and held out her hand. I gave her three twenties, "That's for these two, and one more for him. The change is yours."

She smiled, "Thanks!" She took his empty and replaced it.

"What have you got for me?" David asked after she walked away.

"Missing teenager." I grabbed the cash, and the list of names, from my pocket with Jennifer's social security number written at the bottom. "Your department ruled her a runaway, but the mom wants to be sure the girl's alive."

David took the list, glanced at it, and shoved it in his pocket. "I'm sure we ran all of this."

"I know. It never hurts to double check."

"I'll get on it first thing in the morning. You want another drink?"

My glass looked sad and empty, but my wallet sat sadder and emptier in my pocket. "Can't afford it. I gotta work tonight anyway."

"Come on, Gavin. I'll buy the next round."

Who could say no to that?

Three rounds later, David flicked my ear to get my attention from the stripper in my lap. "Don't you have to work?" He laughed.

"Three sons of half a dozen bitches!"

"Don't go, cutie," said Ginger as she gyrated her hips against my hard-working zipper.

She had a valid point; I am cute as hell. I knew Crystal had nothing to hide. That damn Hank just wanted to clear his conscience by catching her doing something. There's no way he could tell if I didn't actually make it out. The story was the same every time, I was just going stick to it.

"You gonna buy one more round, David?"

"At least!" He laughed again.

I looked Ginger right in the nipples, "I'll be here for a while longer, beautiful."

"Yay!" She clapped and bounced around long enough for me to forget what we had been talking about.

5 HUNGOVER

The sunlight flooding in through David's living room window split my head open like an axe. I kept my eyes closed, but the light turned my eyelids yellow and pink. The Sun is an inconsiderate bastard..

I gave in and sat up. A naked girl was laid there with me, sleeping at the other end of the couch. I rummaged through my pants, which were lying on the floor, until I found a cigarette. Everything smelled like sweat and sex and stale whiskey. Another fun night I couldn't remember.

About halfway through the cigarette, I decided I should put my pants on. They were booze-stained and covered in glitter, but they slid on soft and comfortable. My stomach growled and I couldn't remember eating anything the day before, so I went to the fridge. There, I found a note scrawled on a piece of lined paper, attached to the fridge by a plastic cow magnet.

Gavin-

I had to go to work. Fuck you for sleeping in. Get these girls out of my apartment and don't let them steal anything. Then you can get the hell out too. I'll call you when I get the info you wanted.

Girls? I looked around the living room and kitchen and still only saw the one girl. After a minute of searching, though, I found another girl sleeping in David's bed. She had a tattoo on her bare shoulder that read "Ginger." That seemed familiar.

My stomach growled again. I made myself a couple of scrambled eggs and a cup of instant coffee that I found in the cupboard. After breakfast, I woke the girls up, offered to shower with them (they declined), and ushered them out of the building. Once they were gone; I made sure I had all of my own crap, locked the door, and walked out into the daylight.

Damn it.

My Jeep was still at the strip club. Another good start to another good morning. No way in hell could I walk, feeling the way I did. I called up one of the cab companies in my contact list and told the operator where I would be.

I lucked out and got the only cabbie in the world who didn't want to talk my ear off. I dozed, and before I knew it, we were in the parking lot with my Jeep, and another car which sat patiently waiting for its hungover owner as well. I gave the guy a ten, and told him to keep the change. He pulled away from the lot looking pissed.

I drove home, turned my phone to silent, and slept until the next morning.***

Frustration writhed like a pit of snakes in his stomach as he walked down the stairs toward the basement. They had spent their first night together, with everything going as it should. Jennifer ate his offering, and then he bathed in the warmth of her fear and revulsion once she learned where her meal had come from. The first nights were always perfect.

Since then, though, the girl had shown no fear, no anger, nothing. It had been four nights since her last meal, and she hadn't asked for food or spoken any other word to him. No one had ever made it past three nights without asking, begging for food. When the fourth night came and went, without any give from his newest *lover*, he knew it he needed to move forward.

As the heavy, steel door slid open, a shaft of light crossed the room and fell across Jennifer's face. She was pale, gaunt after days with nothing but water to sustain her young body. He couldn't let it continue or she would starve to death, and that would be a terrible waste.

"Good morning, *lover*," he said as he got the apron and gloves from his storage closet. Her eyes were open, but her face portrayed nothing. He watched her closely as he readied himself for the day's activities. Once his gloves were on, he walked to the sink and began sifting through the blades that were soaking in the basin of acetone. To get her cooperation, to finally bring her to his side, he would need something large for effect, and something sharp to make her first time go smoothly.

"It's not polite to ignore my greeting," he said as he lifted the bone saw into her field of vision. He never used it, didn't like damaging the bones, but it worked well for garnering the response he wanted.

Jennifer's eyes went wide, bunching her brows into a knot beneath the head strap that kept her from moving around on the bed. She squeaked, and he felt his pulse speed up. Fresh tears began washing away the salty streaks that had covered her face since that first night. He couldn't help the smile as it grew wide on his face.

She didn't know about the scalpel, the paring knife, and the needle that he had dropped into the front pocket of his apron. Those were the real tools for the day, and he couldn't wait to use them.

"Please don't..."

"Ahh, so you *can* talk to me, if you want to." He was turned on; blood rushed south and he felt almost light headed. "You've been obstinate the last few days, I feared you may have gone mute."

"Pleeease, let me go home," she whined.

"Do you remember that word, Jennifer? Obstinate? I believe I used it the first time I ever gave you detention. You were being obstinate in my class, something I hope will not continue on in my home."

She stared, doing her best to track him as he moved around the room, without turning her head. She looked on as he pushed a metal cart up to the side of the bed, and poured something clear from a gallon jug, into a steel bowl.

"Mr... Mr. Williamson... Why are you doing this?" she asked, panicked and on the verge of screaming.

"Well, Jennifer, I have to assume that you are famished. At least as hungry as I am; more, since I ate dinner last night. Tonight, I'm going to prepare a special meal for us." He smiled as he stuck the hypodermic needle into her calf. She jumped, but only bent the needle. Her legs were bound too securely for her to do any real damage.

"What are you doing?!"

"Hush, *lover.* I'm only giving you a tiny bit of anesthetic, to keep you from passing out on me." She began to thrash and cuss and beg, but he no longer heard her. The familiar hum rose expectantly in his eardrums as his blood began to boil. It was almost time. First the pain and the begging, the fear, and then later, it would be time for dinner. He couldn't wait to see her take the first bite of her own deliciously cooked flesh. He decided he liked to watch them eat it just as much as he enjoyed eating it himself.

"PLLEEEEASE!!" she screamed, fighting with all she had to look down, to see what he was doing to her leg. He knew she couldn't feel anything, but the terror of not knowing had to be as painful as the cuts.

"Ssshhhh..." he said as he gripped her left calf muscle and readied the scalpel. He only needed eight ounces. With the potatoes and the spinach puffs, eight ounces would be plenty for both of them. His mouth watered as the blade split the skin on her leg for the first time. Blood poured out, soaking into the sheets and filling his senses with its coppery

seduction. The flesh beneath shone out red and
purple and succulent, and gave way easily before the
tiny blade. He cut down and around the fibula,
and began carving out the muscle and tendons
between the fibula and the tibia. There were a couple
of nasty pops as the tendons fell away and a spurt of
warm, thick blood hit his plastic apron and dripped
loudly onto the saturated sheet.

"Please stop..." her voice faded in and out.

"I'm almost done, my love," he said as he used
the paring knife to scrape the last of the muscle from
the exposed bone beneath it. It was challenging to be
precise with the blood rushing to fill the area over and
over again, but he had been here many times
before. "There, all finished. Didn't hurt a bit, did
it?" He stood up, smiling, and dropped both
blades into a pan of acetone on the table. In his left
hand he gingerly held a chunk of the girl's flesh, still
warm. He could feel the blood seeping between the
fingers of his glove.

"I wanna go home..."

"Get some sleep. I'll go prepare dinner."

"I'm not hungry."

"Oh yes you are, and you'll eat every bite or
things are going to get harder for you," his voice took
on a darker edge as he spoke.

"I'm sorry..." she sobbed. Her eyes were glazed
and falling closed, she looked lost and terrified. Her
pain exhilarated him.

He walked out of the room, and up the stairs
into the kitchen, happy for the first time in days.

6 CONTACTS

After sleeping for almost fifteen hours, I felt like a new man. I took a shower, ate a real breakfast, and smoked half a pack of cigarettes before I decided to look at my phone. It wasn't as bad as I expected. Yvette had called half a dozen times to yell at me. Rachel had called twice, maybe to do the same. David had sent me a few texts filled with impolite language, letting me know that he had my "damn information" and that I had better call him ASAP.

I also had some emails full of porn that I decided to save for later.

David first.

The phone rang until it went to voicemail, I hung up. Called again, voicemail again. Called again, "You shitbag, I'm not answering for a reason."

"Oh hey, buddy."

"I'm at a crime scene right now."

"Ooh, something juicy?"

"You have no idea."

"Can you make it to lunch at one?"

"Yeah. That place with the huge ass burritos."

"Good choice."

David hung up. I poured a fresh cup of coffee. The phone rang, a country song. Hank.

"Hello."

"So?" he asked, sounding breathless.

"So what?"

"I had to run out of a shoot to call you, I've got to get back."

"Nothing. Again. She's a goddamn saint."

A moment of silence. "Fine. You coming up today?"

"Not today, I have some work to catch up on."

"Later."

Hank hung up. I took a drink of my coffee, lit a cigarette, and stared at Rachel's name on my contact list.

"Be professional. Don't think about her lips." Great, I had resorted to talking to myself. "Don't think about her legs. No tits or ass. Just business." *Yeah, that's likely.* I hit the green button next to her name.

Same garbage music, then, "Hey, Gavin."

Why did she have to keep saying my name? Didn't she know what that did to me?

"Good morning, Rachel." Good. Short. Professional.

"Any news?"

"Not yet, I just saw that you called. I'm gonna go meet with my contact for lunch, find out what he came up with."

Quiet. Then, a sigh. "Alright."

"I'll let you know whatever I turn up."

"Thanks, Gavin."

Again. I fought back the urge to ask what she was wearing, somehow.

"No problem."

I got to the restaurant before David, ordered two huge-ass burritos, and looked through the papers I had on Jennifer until he showed up. All the pictures and papers were the same, but I stared and flipped them over and over as if it might change something.

"Oh good," David said as he sat across from me. "I love these things. Jesus, you should be glad you didn't see the mess at that scene. This chick was flayed, like to the bone, up and down her arms and legs. Her ass, and even her goddamn ribs. The geek on scene said she must have been alive for most of it."

I pushed my plate away.

"Not eating?" He shoved his fork through the burrito until green chilies oozed through the tortilla. He took a bite three times too large for his mouth. It made my stomach lurch.

"Did you get everything I asked for?" I did my best not to stare at the food sloshing around in his open mouth.

He chewed half a dozen times and swallowed hard. "Yeah, I brought it. It's all there in the original reports, though."

"I figured that." Damn.

"The dad's in prison, you know that?"

"Yeah."

"What are you gonna do?"

"Go through the normal hoops, talk to the people on the list. Waste everyone's time."

"Shitty. If you're not going to eat, do you mind if I split?"

He packed both burritos in one Styrofoam take out carton and I followed David out. We chatted while we had a smoke, and then I drove home. I needed to make some calls.

"Hello, my name is Gavin English. I believe Rachel Davis may have told you I would be calling."

"About Jennifer, right?"

"That's right, can I speak with..."

..."James?"

..."Becky?"

..."Stephanie?"

..."Rick?"

..."Lucy?"

"Sure, just a second. Lucy! Phone for you."

Made sure I had the same list of questions ready to go for the umpteenth time.

"Hi, hello?" She made wet chewing sounds and attempted to speak between bites. Absolutely awful.

"Hi, Lucy?"

"That's me."

"My name is Gavin English. I need to ask you a few questions about your friend, Jennifer."

She stopped chewing. "Oh. You're the guy Jenny's mom told us about. Have you heard anything yet?"

"I'm afraid not, but I'm still considering a few things. I'm staying positive; you should too." Talking to teenage girls was my weak spot. I hated to hear them cry, and arguing or dealing with them angry made it worse. You never knew how it would go.

"Yeah. I'm trying. I miss her."

"Alright, Lucy, I have to start by asking if you have any idea where Jennifer might have been planning to go if she decided to run away."

"No."

"Honestly? You girls never talked about it? Lots of kids do."

"No. We never did. After Denise took off... Well, we didn't want to do that to our friends, you know?"

"Yeah, I get that." *What?!* "Lucy, who's Denise?"

"She used to hang out with us, at school and stuff."

"And she went missing? When was that?"

"Last year. I think she went to her dad's place."

"Oh. You think she did, or you're sure she did?"

"That's what her mom said. She said Denise had been threatening to go to him for a long time. The cops couldn't find him, they told her she was probably right."

This bit of news did not improve my mood. They *were* probably right, it happened every day, but this is something Rachel should have told me.

I ran through the gamut of generic missing persons questions with Lucy after that. Everything else went as routinely as possible: she named off her friends, talked about Jennifer's love life and grades, and cried a little when she admitted she didn't think Jennifer would run away.

I did my best to comfort her, and got off the phone as quickly as possible. My battery was low, I needed a cigarette, and I *desperately* needed to figure

out a nice way of telling Rachel that I hadn't found a
thing.

Phone went off, a text message from
Hank. "Same time tonight."

7 THE BAT, THE BLUE LABEL, AND THE BELL

Etta James poured through my speakers when Crystal's Cadillac backed out of the driveway. I only waited a few seconds to give her a lead, and then drove onto the street. In the darkness I could just make out her rear license plate, "PANKY." I didn't need two guesses to figure out what his plate would say.

The woman kept in good shape, and not by accident. She worked out hard and she worked out a lot. I'm not ashamed to admit that I've thought of more than a couple scenarios where I let her know that Hank sent me to follow her, and she rewards me in the best, dirtiest ways possible.

As I tailed her through a few intersections, I guessed that we were heading to one of the gyms on the west side. The city was bursting with busy professionals who sneak their workouts in after hours.

However, there's a certain street in Reno that runs under the freeway. There *are* professionals who work on that street after dark, but they don't do it in a gym. I almost didn't notice when I followed the Cadillac right onto that street. Almost. Then, a thousand bells went off in my booze-soaked mind. What the hell would she be doing around here?

I had to drop back even more if I hoped to remain unnoticed with no traffic on this street at night aside from the occasional taxi or drunk driver sneaking home. When I could only see her taillights, I picked up speed. I watched as she turned into several parking lots, only to come right back out and continue down the street. She must have been looking for something specific, maybe someone uncircumcised. Or a midget. Or she could have been picking up people at each stop.

Now that was an intriguing thought. If she was cheating, I couldn't see any reason not to try and get a little action myself. She might even be dirty enough for me to remember it the next day.

I stopped once again as she pulled into another lot. One minute went by. Two. She didn't come back out. I cruised up the road until I could see her Cadi. I parked across the street, shut off the lights, and got out my camera.

Crystal stood next to her SUV, talking on the phone. I couldn't hear her side of the conversation, but she was animated and angry, waving her arms around and spitting while she talked. When she finished, she stuffed the phone back into the pocket of her fashionable, ass-shaping yoga pants, and opened the back door.

Curiouser and curiouser.

When she shut the door again she had a Louisville Slugger in her hand. For a second, I thought I had been made and that I might have to speed away with a crazed woman chasing me up the street. Then I saw something that made me laugh. A couple of spots down from her Cadillac I saw a huge pickup truck with a license plate that read, "HANKY." Thank you, Carrie Underwood, for inspiring pissed off women everywhere.

The next five minutes were a blast. For me anyway; I'm pretty sure Hank's truck did not have fun. Crystal took that venerable slugger to the man's windshield and several of his windows. She broke the headlights and the taillights, and left a couple dozen good-sized dents and dings all over the truck's body. By the end of it, she was sweaty and smiling and I had at least thirty new pictures on my phone.

I saved the pics and pulled up Hank's number in my address book.

"What's up, Gavin?" he yelled over the sound of pumping hip hop music.

"Have you talked to Crystal tonight?" I tried hard not to laugh as she climbed back into her SUV and drove off.

Hank chuckled, "Yeah, she called a while ago bitchin' about something or another. Why, what's up?"

"I only asked because it looks like she's heading back home."

"Nothing then?" I swear I heard disappointment and a stripper sweating.

"She's clean, Hank."

"Bull."

Hank hung up and I put the phone in my pocket. I took another minute to enjoy the damage Crystal had left behind before turning the Jeep around and heading back to civilization. Before I reached the overpass, my phone rang.

I dug it back out, doing my best not to swerve from my lane, "Gavin English."

"What are you up to tonight?" David asked, sounding like he was in a good mood.

"I'm cruising Fourth Street right now, why?"

"Dirty pervert," he laughed. "Pay your hooker and come get a drink with me."

"The Rail?"

"Yeah, I'll be there in fifteen. Don't make me wait for-fucking-ever this time."

I put the phone down after he hung up and braved a quick sniff under my pits. Not bad, half deodorant, half manly musk. No need to head home and change. I may not have been dressed up, but at least I wasn't wearing sweats this time.

With it being a weeknight, I didn't have to pay to get in to the strip club, but the bouncer gave me the hairy eyeball as I walked by for good measure. He's probably dating one of the strippers we took home the other night. Oh well, not the first time, won't be the last.

David sat at the bar with two full tumblers of something dark in front of him, and a girl pressing her cleavage as close to his face as she could without letting him motorboat her. Her voice came out sultry and sweet and she kept touching his arm and mussing his hair until he told her that he wasn't interested in a private dance. She took off quickstyle, and forgot that he existed.

"Keeping up your winning streak with the ladies I see," I said as I dropped down on the stool next to him.

"Yeah yeah, go to hell." He turned and looked me up and down, "Jesus, you might as well be wearing sweats. You look like hot garbage."

"I wish you'd stop calling me Jesus. And back off; I've been working, what's your excuse?"

He laughed and emptied his glass in one shot. "Speaking of work, we had a big day today."

"Oh yeah?" I asked, taking my first swig from my glass. The liquid tasted spicy and smooth, better than our usual. Delicious even. "Woah, what's with the Blue Label?"

"I told you, big day at work! We got an ID on that girl from the other day, the one who was all cut up."

"Okay, well that's good news, but why the hell are you so happy?"

"That douchebag, Rodriguez, got hammered by the news all day, and the Captain made him step down."

It didn't make any sense. Why would the Lieutenant get in trouble for getting an ID on a murder victim? "You're gonna have to give me more if you want me to play along," I said before finishing off my tasty drink.

"Rodriguez handled the missing persons case last year, filed this girl as a runaway and shoved the whole thing down the line so he could move on to bigger and better. Almost no investigation, and no follow-up at all."

The Blue Label started fighting bells in the back of my head, something about the girl. I didn't want to think too hard. When choosing sides, I always went with the booze. There was *something* there though.

"We're celebrating because Rodriguez is getting taken down a peg? I can get behind that," I joked as I shook my empty glass at him.

"No! We're celebrating because I'm getting the bump to Lieutenant! Jackass."

I smiled and raised my empty glass, "That's amazing. Congrats, David. You deserve it. So, this Jane Doe is gonna be your first case as L.T.?"

"Damn right, but she's not a Jane Doe. First thing tomorrow, I gotta find out everything I can about Denise Beckham. Tonight, though, I'm getting drunk as a skunk so I can spend all the extra cash I'm making."

That damn bell started niggling at the back of my consciousness again. This time, the Blue Label lost out. "Did you say her name was Denise?"

The bartender set two more glasses in front of David, and he took his down in one swallow. After a booze shiver, he answered, "Yeah, Denise Beckham. A local girl who went missing about a year ago. Why?"

"Shit." It could be a coincidence, most likely the situations were unrelated, but the girls knew each other. "I think I just had a conversation about her with one of the kids on the list my client gave me."

"About Denise? You talked to someone that knew her?" David got a pen from his breast pocket and reached for the napkin under his empty glass. "Give me the name and number."

I needed to call Rachel. This could mean the P.D. would take both cases, and work them together. Or it could mean nothing. My brain fluttered with new information and Johnnie Walker Blue.

"Her name was Lucy, but all the rest is back at my place. My girl and your girl were close, them and Lucy."

"How long has your girl been missing?"

"A week or so."

"It's worth looking into..." David belched and stared into his empty glass for several seconds. "You know what? I'm not working tonight. Let's have fun right now, and we can put our heads together tomorrow. I'll see if I can bring you on, advisory capacity or something."

He wanted to be nice, but we both knew there was no way in Hell the P.D. would let me in on the investigation. In any capacity. When I quit, the Captain and I did not part ways gracefully. Shit.

"Thanks, Dave, but I better take off. You have a great time tonight, get a couple lap dances for me."

"Seriously? Come on, how often am I in a good enough mood to invite you out, and pay for drinks?"

"Sorry. I'll call you tomorrow with Lucy's number."

One of the newer girls found her way onto David's lap and he waved me off. She was cute, too young to feel good about taking home, but cute. I had a spasm of jealousy as the bartender refilled David's glass again and made a hasty exit before I could change my mind.

The temperature outside had dropped a few degrees and the evening air helped clear my mind with each breath. I stretched and let the chill do its work on my head. I had to look at those papers again. And in the morning, I needed to get to David before his hangover cleared up. Maybe he would let me check out the files on the cut up girl, *if* I could get to it before his better sense kicked in.

I lit up a fresh cigarette and stared at my Jeep. She looked lonely, but I knew the drinks still had me foggy and slow. Across the parking lot I spotted a cab just waiting for some horny drunk guy to need a ride home. The sign on top might as well have read, "Gavin, get your ass in here, drunky, and give us your money."

8 BREAKFAST TIME

I couldn't sleep. I drank enough to have a wicked headache before the sun got a chance to rise, but not enough to help me get to dreamland. My head just wouldn't turn off. Could the girls' situations be related? Did that mean that Jennifer was getting filleted at that moment? And in the more selfish region of my mind, I worried that this would mean that the case, and my fare, would be handed to the P.D.

To hell with that.

I sat up and grabbed my phone, scrolling to Rachel's number in my contact list and hitting the green call button. I doubted that she would be awake so early, but this needed to be done.

To my horror, I realized that I already knew most of the words to the terrible song that replaced her ringer. Before it could cut to voicemail, she answered with incoherent mumbling.

"Rachel, it's Gavin."

I heard a bed creak and a few other sounds that you should only hear from a person when you know them intimately. For a long time. "What is it, Gavin? Did you find something?" I could tell she was trying to clear her head and not to be annoyed at the same time.

"Maybe not. But I have to talk to you. Can you meet me for breakfast in half an hour?"

"I don't... What is...? Yeah. That's fine."

"Alright, I'll meet you at the Denny's off Plumb."

"Are they even open at 2am?"

"They're always open."

I arrived before Rachel and ordered all the coffee they had available. The waitress laughed and brought me a glass of ice water and the tiniest white porcelain tea cup I had ever seen, half full of coffee.

"I'm gonna need at least eight of those. Or bring one of your pots to the table."

She forced a smile, still not sure if I was kidding, "Umm, seriously?"

"Yes. Please." To make my point I slammed the entire cup in one shot. It burned. Everything from my gums to my guts were on fire and I couldn't be sure if I would ever use my tongue again. The waitress's eyes went wide and I gave her the biggest smile I could, doing my best to hide the agony that I had forced on myself.

She walked away stiffly and came back with one of those old-fashioned glass pots that had the big, black plastic handle. "Can I get you anything else?"

Not daring to speak with my tongue still boiling in my mouth, I shook my head. Once she turned away I reached into the ice water, grabbed as many cubes as I could, and shoved them into my mouth. They melted almost immediately, and I had to fight to swallow.

This is why I shouldn't be allowed to make decisions, or interact with the general public, before I have coffee.

After a few minutes, the burning subsided and I could drink at a normal speed. Other than a scratchy, sore tongue, I would make a full recovery. The pain, mixed with copious amounts of caffeine, cleared the remaining Blue Label from my head by the time Rachel arrived.

She sat in the bench seat across from me, looking great, despite being woken up so early. Her hair sat high and tight in a ponytail, and she wasn't wearing any makeup. Even the jeans and sweatshirt she had thrown on accentuated her body perfectly. Goddamn.

"What's with the giant pot of coffee?"

"I don't know, the waitress dropped it off when I got here. I think she's lazy."

"Figures. What did you want to talk about?"

All I *wanted* to talk about was the possibility of us getting some naked snuggle time in before the sun came up. Maybe I could bring it up after.

"Are you hungry? Want some coffee?"

"No. I want to get this over with so that I can go back to bed and get a little more sleep before I go to work at 6am."

"Right." No reason not to dive right in then, I guess. "How well did you and your daughter know Denise Beckham?"

Her face changed, sad, thoughtful. "She was great. We were both heart broken when she went off with her dad. It may have been for the best though, her mom... well, she had issues at home. Jennifer didn't go to Denise, did she?"

I knew how to break bad news to people, and had done it many times in the past. As a cop, or as a private investigator, bad news came as part of the job. That didn't mean I liked it, or that I had any level of skill when it came to softening the blow. I took a thin, slow sip from my cup to bide time before answering, "Denise's case has been reopened. She may not have run away from home after all."

Rachel knew what I was building up to. She closed her eyes and breathed deep. When she opened them back up, she did her best not to look at me. "What happened?"

"I'm sorry, Rachel. Denise's body turned up a couple of days ago, here in town."

Tears. I never know how to deal with people crying. I can't look at them because I don't want them to feel embarrassed, but I can't look away without seeming like a heartless dick. I did my best to look solemn and find that space between giving her room to grieve and being there for comfort. Pretty sure I failed. At all of it.

"I can't believe she's gone," she said with a handful of wadded up napkins over her mouth. "When Jennifer finds out..." I watched as the realization hit her. It was quick. From mourning to scared shitless in zero-point-four seconds.

"We're not sure it means anything yet, Rachel," I did my best to stop her from exploding in a frightened-mother-angry-beast-sad-ball of lava. "It's been quite a while since Denise went missing, and her case and your daughter's are not likely to be connected."

Her eyes turned dull as she accepted something I will never know about, and she wiped the tears from her face. "But they could be. Right?"

If I were still in uniform there would be a protocol for this. Give non-answers, keep it vague until everything is set in stone. But I didn't wear a uniform anymore, and I wasn't going to lie to a missing girl's mother.

"Yes. They could be connected. My friend on the force asked me to share the list of names and numbers that you gave me. I expect you'll be contacted before the end of the day." The smells of the restaurant suddenly hit me. Bacon and eggs and ham and burnt toast and a hundred other things that made my stomach lurch. "Want to go outside for some fresh air?"

She nodded and stood up. I threw a fiver on the table and followed as she made her way out. Outside, the sun remained elusive, but the black sky had turned navy blue, and the chill faded from the air.

"I'm going to do everything I can to help out, but I'm sure the police are going to take over before long."

"Why? They didn't want to do anything before. What's different now?"

"The information has changed, Rachel. They have good people who will look into this, find out where she is."

"What about you?"

"Like I said, I'll do everything I can until they take over. Maybe, I can find something that will point them in the right direction."***

Jennifer woke up with no idea how long she had slept. Her stomach clenched and writhed in her abdomen, waiting to burst. When she had last been awake, she ate the dinner her old English teacher had prepared for her. Every bit of it. She blinked the sleep out of her eyes and found him there, wearing that awful smile and sitting across the table from her.

He insisted that she call him "*lover*," and made her promise to eat all her food before he would unstrap her from the bed. After she agreed, he bandaged her leg, packing it with something that smelled rancid but felt cool against her inflamed flesh.

Then he helped her to a small bathroom hidden behind a metal closet in the room, and nursed her through a shower. Although he wasn't shy about touching her, he didn't seem to get any pleasure out of it. That didn't stop Jennifer from cringing whenever their skin made contact.

Afterward, he dressed her in oversized nurse's scrubs and led her upstairs, to a well-lit dining room. After days without food, the smells that greeted her made her salivate and her knees nearly gave out from the hunger. Mr. Williamson sat her at the lavish wooden dining table, and strapped her upper thighs and waist to the chair.

"Now we can enjoy a proper meal together," he said as he slid a plate full of food in front of her. "You'll see there is no need to be rude or selfish here, *lover*."

She ate the potatoes, and some soft pastries that tasted like cheese. Her body soaked the food in and she didn't think she would ever get full. He allowed her to refill her plate several times before he began to stare at the portion she kept skipping over.

"You'll have to finish it all if you don't want to go several more days without eating."

"I don't know if I can." She remembered the fear, the disgust as she looked down at the seared meat on her plate. It smelled divine, but that made it worse. She decided that perhaps an offering would help, something that showed she wasn't angry, that she wouldn't be obstinate anymore. "I wouldn't mind if you had my bit... *lover.*"

"No!" He stood up and slammed his fist down on the table, knocking over her glass of water and making her jump hard enough that it might have torn the bandage from the wound on her leg. "I cooked that piece for you, Jennifer. I expect you to be grateful. I expect you to do as you promised. Now."

With her lips trembling and tears welling up in her eyes, her entire body convulsing, she stabbed the leg meat with her fork and began cutting it. Each time she moved the knife, she remembered how helpless and weak she had felt, tied to the bed as he sliced into her calf without pause. She sobbed and gagged over and over until the meat was spread out in tiny pieces across her plate.

"Good," he stated, his voice full of sugar, "now eat it." Her mouth watered and her stomach trundled up and down, threatening to send everything back where it came from. With one last look into his soulless eyes, she jammed the first bite into her mouth. She fought to swallow it whole, couldn't imagine having to chew, but her body refused to participate in what was happening. She vomited in her mouth and only just kept it from spewing out onto the table. She breathed through her nose and did her best to imagine that she was eating anything else in the entire world. Jennifer forced herself to swallow back each gag until her mouth came away empty and dry.

That had been the first of eighteen pieces she had to force down. Each bite, just as difficult as the first, and she had several close calls which surely would have ended badly for her. She didn't want to imagine how angry he would get if she threw up even the smallest amount.

Now, hours later, or days, she didn't know which, her body betrayed her again. She pressed the buzzer switch, which he had taped to her hand, three times, and then waited.

After several minutes, the door to the staircase opened and Mr. Williamson walked in.

"What do you need, love? I'm about to head off to work."

She wanted to scream and rail and fight and curse, but the only words she could manage were, "I'm hungry... *lover.*"

"Oh good, I have a fruit plate prepared for you, and enough time for us to enjoy breakfast before I have to leave for work."

A fruit plate? It was too good to be true, yet she smiled as he undid the straps from her head, chest, wrists, waist, and knees. "That sounds delicious."

9 LIES AND OMISSIONS

It was almost noon and I still hadn't heard from David about bringing him Lucy's info. Maybe I got lucky and he forgot. That would buy me extra time, but then I wouldn't have any shot at seeing the files on Denise. What a clusterfuck.

I'd spent the morning memorizing every line, every picture, and every name in the papers that Rachel had given me. So far, I had come up with nothing new. After a pack and a half of smokes, and three pots of coffee, I decided that I might do more good by leaving the house.

After a shower and a shave, I called Jennifer and Denise's school. A woman, who must have been a smoker since the Old Testament answered the office phone, "Principal's office."

"Hi there, I was hoping to make an appointment to speak with someone about Denise Beckham." By now the faculty had to know that the police were reopening the case. Hopefully, someone from the department hadn't already called. If I could be the first one in, I could slide right through without anyone questioning me.

"Oh. Dear, yes. The poor girl. I'm sure Mr. Rawlings will make room for you. What time did you want to come in Officer...?"

"You can call me Gavin. Gavin English. Would it be alright if I swung by in about twenty minutes?"

"That sounds fine. Mr. Rawlings will be off of lunch by then."

"Thank you."

"They call me Lenore around here, dear."

"Thank you, Lenore."

After I hung up the phone, I scrounged in my closet to find something to wear. It's been my experience that if you walk around in something nice, and act like you're allowed to be anywhere you want, people don't question it. Over the last few years, I've purchased two Armani suits: one for special occasions, silky and cut just right to accentuate my chest and ass, and one for official business, flat, charcoal and straight cut as can be. It looked as good on me as the first one, but it was loose enough in the shoulders and chest that I could carry my piece without anyone knowing.

After I laid out the suit on my bed, I slid my gun safe out of the closet and unlocked it. I don't like guns, never have, which always made people ask me why I became a cop. I don't see what the two have to do with each other. A soft dislike of firearms, however, did not stop me from seeing that it's essential to protect myself in my line of work. It would be awesome to walk around with a battle-axe strapped to your back, but how the hell will you get seated at a restaurant like that?

A smooth, black Makarov 9x18 millimeter hung snug and cozy in my shoulder holster, though. No problem getting a table with that. I lifted the gun from its case and pulled and released the chamber to ensure that it wasn't loaded. It isn't like I go to the gun range daily, but I always go with safety first when dealing with something that can kill me. It was clear, and the magazine filled, so I locked the safety, loaded it, and clipped it into my holster.

The top button on the jacket pulled a bit tighter than the last time I'd worn it so I made a mental note to get back to the gym. Once I suited up, I straightened out my hair, threw on a dab of smell-good, and rushed out of there. I had work to do, and not a lot of time to do it in.

As soon as lunch time ends, and traffic on the freeway is all asses and elbows. I was thinking about pulling my gun to make room for myself when my phone started to vibrate and sing in my breast pocket.

"Yeah?"

"Gavin, Jesus Christ I got a headache. You should've stuck around, man. We partied and drank and half the bar came home with me last night."

Good time to get responsible, huh. "Good for you, Dave. You calling to rub my nose it?"

"No, man. I wanted you to buy me a congratulatory lunch and bring that chick's number for me."

"Yeah, sounds good. But I'm in the middle of something right now, is a late lunch okay with you?"

"Sure, I'm the boss now remember?"

"Hey, can I ask you a favor too?" I had to play this part carefully if I wanted any shot at seeing those files.

"What's up?"

"Do you think there's any chance I could see the stuff you got on the Beckham girl? Before your uniforms steal my fare?"

"Uhh, I don't know, Gav..."

"You don't have to leave them with me or anything, just let me get a look. Maybe take down a few notes?"

"Alright, since you're helping me out. Sure."

Couldn't have gone better if it I had been writing the script. Things were falling in line in a way that made me sure that the shit was about to hit the fan. Oh well. No reason to miss the party because you're afraid of a hangover.

I arrived at the school after 1pm; the grounds were silent and I parked near the front entrance. I jumped out of the Jeep, straightened my suit, and headed for the front office. The room was clinical. Off-white walls, inspirational posters everywhere, and only one clock, right above the principal's office so that people didn't drive themselves crazy staring at it all day.

"Can I help you?" came the same smoke scarred voice from the phone.

"Lenore?"

"Yes, are you the policeman I spoke with?"

I gave my winningest smile, "Gavin English, that's me."

Lenore leaned over a twenty-year-old push-button phone and hit the intercom button with an arthritic finger. "Mr. Rawlings, Officer English is here to see you."

"*Send him right in*," came a man's voice through the speaker which made it sound like he was yelling down a hallway full of air conditioners.

"Go ahead, dear," said Lenore. She pointed to the closed office door beneath the clock.

"Thanks, Lenore."

Rawlings' door was heavy, like he wanted to make sure people couldn't get in or out without him knowing. I guess high school principals never change; mine was a sadistic bastard too. He didn't get up to greet me, just waved me in and pointed to a short chair directly across the desk from him. Typical passive aggressive power play; I didn't like this guy.

"Hello, Officer English. How can we help you?"

I leaned against the chair rather than sitting down, "Please, call me Gavin. I'm here because I'd like to ask you a few questions about Denise Beckham."

He shook his head and forced on a sad face. "It's a tragedy. Of course, we've all been keeping up with the news. I've seen that you boys in the department are taking a lick over the whole thing too, huh?"

"Oh, you know the police department; can't even be sure who's working there half the time." We shared a laugh. We were both faking. "It's been a while, but I was wondering what you might be able to tell me about Denise."

"She was somewhere in the middle, to be perfectly honest with you. Grades were average, ditched an average amount of school, and got into a little more than average trouble. Unfortunately, with as many kids as we have here, I can't have a close relationship with all of them."

"Right. What about her friends, anything or anyone who you can think of that might be a help?"

He shook his head again, making his extra chins jiggle beneath his short salt and pepper beard. "As far as I know, they were all quite alike. She hung around with that other girl, the one who ran away last week. And a few others who have been in and out of my office from time to time."

I took out a pen and my official-looking notebook and scribbled a picture of a dick on it. He raised his eyes to sneak a peek. I flipped it closed. "About Denise, you say she got in more than the usual trouble. Tell me about that."

"Nothing major, nothing involving the police or anything like that. She was a frequent flyer. She didn't like some faculty members, and had no problem mouthing off. She and a couple of the other girls were removed from one class for constant insubordination."

I opened my notebook again, scribbled down the first line of the Pledge of Allegiance to make it look official, and closed it. "Could you tell me the names of the girls?"

He flipped open a brown file folder that had been sitting on his desk. "It looks like Lucy Taylor and Jennifer Davis. She ran away last year."

No new names, but I definitely needed to get back in touch with Lucy. I flipped open my notebook again, "Which teacher did they have trouble with? The one who removed them from class?"

"Looks like Mr. Williamson. English teacher." Probably another dead end, but at least I had an actual name to write down.

"What about fighting, were there any students that she didn't get along with?"

"They all fight. I can't even begin to keep track of that, unless there is a real altercation. With Denise, there are none in my files."

Something made an awful buzzing noise that almost made me drop my very official notebook. It was the intercom.

"*Mr. Rawlings, there is another policeman here to speak with you about Denise.*"

Rawlings raised his eyebrow in my direction, "Expecting reinforcements?"

For once, I had nothing to say. I gave a tiny nod, shoved my notebook back into my pocket, and said, "Thanks for your cooperation. I'll see who they sent." I slid out through the dungeon door and did my best to be inconspicuous as I made my way across the office. I saw David chatting with the old lady at the desk. He saw me too.

"I warmed him up for you, buddy," I said with a wink as I made my way out as fast as I could without running.

I didn't even look back to see if he followed me. I would get an earful for this, but I didn't technically do anything wrong. I was following up a lead for a client, so I guessed he'd forgive me by the time we had lunch.

"Hey!" Shit. I had my hand on the Jeep door and I played with the idea of playing deaf. I knew it would never work. I turned with a smile which faltered for a moment when I realized the voice hadn't come from David.

I didn't recognize him, but a tall, thin, balding man walked toward me, waving.

"Yeah?" I asked in my casual, I need to book it the hell out of here, voice.

"The office said that you were investigating Denise Beckham. I hoped you could tell me if you had found anything. We're all kind of waiting with bated breath to see what kind of a monster could do that to a young girl."

"Oh. Sorry, no. I don't know much at this time. And you are?"

He extended a perfectly manicured hand to me, "I'm Robert Williamson. Denise is a student of mine."

I shook his hand. Something about him rubbed me the wrong way, but the guy was a *high school* teacher, and I'd always had a bit of an issue with authority. Still, it's always best to be polite in situations like these, "It's nice to meet you, Mr. Williamson. Were you close with Denise?"

"Oh very," he answered. "She's one of my favorite students, a joy to have in class."

I'm not sure why people think they should lie to cops about the dumbest shit. Not that I was a cop, but he didn't know that. I decided to see if I could poke a few holes and find something new. "I'm glad to hear that, maybe you can help me out. Since you were close to Denise, would you be willing to answer a few questions about her and a couple of her friends for me?"

A flash of something dark crossed his face, gone before I had a chance to get a read on it. He smiled,

"Of course. Anything to help out. I should get back for class right now, but if you have
time tomorrow I'm taking a vacation day to get some yard work done. You're more than welcome to swing by, I'll grill up something tasty and you can ask me all the questions you want."

Was he hitting on me? Either way, he might have information I needed and I had come too far to back out now, "Sounds good." I handed him a page from my notebook and a pen. "If you'll give me your address, I'll be there around noon tomorrow."

10 CUTS AND SLICES

He felt his heart pounding away in his chest, rhythmic and strong, beating a pulse to his brain to set off his fight or flight response. He loved it. There would be no fight or flight, not now. As he left the parking lot behind and made his way through hallway after hallway, he formed a plan. He really felt alive for the first time he could remember in years, but the adrenaline slipped away with each passing second. Returning him to *normal.*

He didn't know Gavin English, but he knew he wasn't a cop. Not a cop, but close enough to be trouble. As far as he knew, no one had ever looked into his... extracurricular activities. He knew to always be careful, always patient. Patience was key. Looking back through a history of people with tastes like his made it clear: If you don't plan, or get rushed, give in to a momentary impulse, then you were likely to be caught.

By the time he reached the classroom the students' voices, their laughing, shushing, and joking sounded like nothing more than a faded buzz at the edge of his attention. Without thinking, he scribbled page numbers on the chalk board and sat in the faded corduroy chair behind his desk. "Read the pages silently," he said. "Tomorrow's scheduled test will be postponed because I will not be in class."***

"Do you know how much shit you'll be in if the school tells Captain Meadows that you were impersonating a cop?" asked David as he slid a greasy slice of pepperoni pizza onto his plate. My place was messy, but I hoped I might worm my way into a glimpse of the crime scene photos. Lunch in a public place seemed like a bad idea.

"I never said I was a cop."

David shook his head, "I'm second guessing my decision to let you see these files. Rodriguez would love to see me fall on my ass in my first week as L.T."

"I'm serious, Dave. I called up, told them my name, told them I was investigating the Denise Beckham case. I can't be held responsible if they jumped to conclusions."

"Goddammit," he replied.

We ate in silence, each of us staring at the other's files, hoping that they might reveal answers we hadn't found yet.

After my second slice, I gave in, "Listen, you haven't connected Denise and Jennifer yet, and neither have I. At this point, we're passing ideas back and forth. Like we've done a hundred times." I slid Rachel's folder across the coffee table as a peace offering. "I'm sorry for stepping on your toes, but I promised Jennifer's mother I would do everything I could to point you in the right direction if the connection turns official. From here on out, I'll pass everything I do by you first."

"Like hell you will," he snorted as he slid his files to me. "I hope you have copies of this shit, I'm keeping it," he said, indicating my folder.

"No worries, boss."

Halfway through my next slice I came to the first crime scene photo taken where they found Denise's body. Appetite officially lost. When David told me the girl had been cut up, it had in no way prepared me for the cruelty in those pics. Denise had been stripped down to bone, in at least a hundred separate places. As the images progressed, I could see that the edges of each cut had been allowed to heal, probably bandaged and cleaned meticulously. Nine strips of flesh from her left leg, seven from her right, each arm had six cuts, and they all went to the bone.

As I studied the shots of her torso, I had to fight to keep my pizza down. "Jesus fucking Christ."

"I'm pretty sure that wasn't his middle name," David chuckled.

"Very funny. What happened here?"

"According to the lab guys, the ribs were stripped one at a time."

"Jesus." The girl's left side was all angry and inflamed flesh, scabbed over and turning gangrenous. Aside from the burnt look of the skin at the edges of the wounds, the right side of her torso looked healthy and untouched. Last, and worst of all, the left side of her skull seemed to have been carved open like the top of a pumpkin.

"This the cause of death?" I asked, holding up the last photo.

"Seems that way. Coroner is still on it. All I know is that there are no signs of rape, and she had a heartbeat up to 24 hours before she got dropped off with the medical examiner."

I put the photos back in the file and closed it. "Lunch was a bad idea."

"You've been out of the game too long, watching old fat guys cheat on their wives isn't very messy," replied David as he picked up another slice with a smile.

"Don't think so? That just means you've never seen fat old guys get naked."

He made a face and put the pizza back in the box. "Thanks, buddy. Now, I'll never get that image out of my head."

"Anytime, Lieutenant."

David smiled and flipped me off, "One big question, though: Why did they stop? Whoever did this, why leave the other side of her chest? If it's a kind of ritual or experiment, I don't get it."

A replay of the pictures ran through my mind. Clean cuts, lots of muscle, no belly cuts, nothing near the pelvis. This wasn't surgery. "The gangrene. That's why the cutting stopped."

"What are you talking about?" he asked as he pulled the file back toward himself.

"Think about it. Making so many cuts, keeping her alive. When the meat gets left out, eventually it starts to turn if you keep it fresh instead of frozen."

"Oh my god." I could see the change in his expression as he caught on to my meaning. "You think she was taken by a cannibal?"

"They killed her because they wanted the brain
before the gangrene could reach the blood. Once
that happened the infection would've spread
quick. Blood, kidneys, heart, and then the
brain. Can't eat the brain if it goes bad. That would
be unhealthy."

11 BLOOD AND STRAWBERRIES

"Honey, I'm home," he said as he entered the basement. His penny loafers padded softly against the concrete floor as he made his way to Jennifer's side. "Exciting day at work, the police were in and out all afternoon."

Jennifer bit her lip to keep from crying. She had been asleep, dreaming about home, making breakfast with her mom and hanging out with Denise and Lucy. Now, she found herself back in a concrete-lined basement that smelled of dried blood and her own piss. "I'm so glad you're home, *lover*."

"Me too." He leaned down and kissed her on the forehead. "I think I may have made a new friend while the police were there."

A glimmer of hope popped up and Jennifer swiftly quashed it before it could do any more damage. There had probably been a fight at school, or a kid showed up with a knife. She had no reason to believe that police at the high school had anything to do with her. "That sounds exciting. *Lover*."

"Oh, it is. I invited him over for lunch tomorrow."

It was almost too much for Jennifer to keep from hoping. There were cops at the school, possibly looking for her, and now they might have another person into the house. There really could be a chance for her in it all, and she didn't think she would be able to keep that thought down.

At least, not until Mr. Williamson said, "Unfortunately, my sweet, this means that I am going to have to break my promise. If I'm going to be entertaining, I am going to need something delicious on the menu."

Despair, somehow worse than before, engulfed Jennifer. Worse, she knew, because she had given in and dared to hope that things might get better. Now her tears flowed unabashedly, and her body shook with the sobbing that came from deep in her chest. For the first time in her life, she truly wanted to die.

"Don't worry!" he exclaimed, now donning his plastic apron and gloves. I'll be sure to make enough so that I can prepare you a plate before he arrives. No time for the needle, though. I need to get the marinade going."

The first cut on her leg still hurt more than anything she had ever felt before being strapped down in the bastard's basement. Now she looked on in horror as he showed her the largest carving knife she had ever seen.

"I'll be quick, love. Don't you worry about passing out if you need to, I won't be offended."

With that, she felt him clamp his gloved hand above her right knee, and then the blade dug into her calf. She screamed so loud she thought she might tear her throat. The pain ripped through her. The knife tore back and forth through her flesh, and she felt the world closing in as her mind began to shut off. She screamed. She screamed until darkness engulfed her consciousness. The last thing she saw was her own blood splattering, like a Rorschach test, on the ceiling above her bed.***

The afternoon came in hot and cloudy, and soon thunderstorms arrived. The rain poured nonstop and the sky exploded with lightning every few minutes. I stayed home and shut off my cell phone so that I could drink the day away. I was running on zero sleep for the week and a morning of questioning the high school gestapo, followed by staring at some sick asshole's long pork leftovers. I couldn't take anymore.

I sat out on the tiny balcony which was afforded to me by my tiny apartment, and poured the last of an old bottle into my glass. The rain washed the urban landscape clean. Maybe that meant something. Maybe things just got dirtier after a while, and a good rain could clean it up. Not only the streets, but the people. Maybe the rain would make this sadistic piece of shit bring Jennifer home and turn himself in. Tomorrow was a new day, after all.

Yeah, I was drunk. Without warning, I found myself with an empty glass in my hand and I headed to the kitchen for a fresh bottle. I still wore my suit pants, but my jacket, shirt, tie, shoulder harness (complete with holster and pistol), and shoes were piled beneath the bar where I had stripped down as soon as I got home. I lifted the bottle of Jameson, a recent and wise purchase, from its brown paper bag and tore the lid off. Took a swig for good measure, poured three fingers into my glass, and wiped the top of the bottle with the edge of my tank top.

As soon I stepped out onto the balcony, the doorbell rang. I set my glass, and the bottle, on the wooden rail, and walked back inside. Mormons and census takers never came by this late in the day, so I decided not to be angry until I actually knew who had decided to break up my solitary drinking night.

"Rachel?"

She nodded and brushed past me into the apartment. "I hope it's okay, I found your address in the yellow pages." Although rain from the storm had soaked her hair and clothes, my keen detective senses told me that she had been crying. Also, she had a handful of damp tissue, and continued crying.

"What are you doing here? Did something happen?"

She took off her stylish leather jacket and laid it on the arm of my couch. "Can I have a drink?"

"Of course." What else could I say? She followed me into the kitchen where I grabbed a clean tumbler out of the cupboard for her. "Ice?"

She shook her head. I took her and the clean glass out onto the balcony, where we sat down and I poured her two fingers worth. She tossed it back, grimaced, and held the glass out to me. I gave her another. This time, she only drank half of it before shivering and putting the glass down.

"Your friend called me today to tell me that they were officially reopening my daughter's case. I didn't even know it was closed. She hasn't been found, so how the hell did they close her case?"

I got two cigarettes from my pack on the ground next to me, lit them both, and handed one to Rachel. "It wasn't closed. He basically meant that rather than posting Jennifer's face on the internet and milk cartons, they are going to treat it as an active investigation."

She took the cigarette and emptied her glass again. I followed suit, and then refilled us both.

"I need to know whether or not she's alive."

"I know."

That thought hung in the air, thicker than the blankets of rain that continuously pounded against the balcony's overhang. For the next hour, we didn't speak. We drank most of the whiskey, and chain-smoked a whole pack of cigarettes while the white noise of the rain pattered and splashed the world around us, but we didn't say a word to each other. She cried off and on and I did my best to comfort her, without breaking the silence. Before I knew it, her head was resting against my chest and I had my arms around her, running my fingers through her hair.

She sat up and wiped the tears from her face, then looked me in the eye. She said a thousand different things with that look, but my mind was too clouded by the booze, the rain, and the smell of her perfume to notice.

Then she kissed me. Hard and fast and before I knew it her tongue slipped between my lips, digging forward until it met with mine. I kissed her back, with one hand buried in her hair and the other navigating its way from her knee, to her thigh and higher. I pressed on until my fingers slid against the warmth of the cotton between her legs.

Somewhere beneath the whiskey and the smoke I could taste strawberries on her lips. She moaned while our tongues were still searching each other and I could feel my cock pressing against the fabric of my pants, aching and swelling more with each second.

Was this happening? I sucked in a mouthful of her breath and pushed away. "Wait. Rachel. You've been drinking. I'm not sure if this..."

She cut me off with a whispered, "Fuck you, Gavin."

"What?"

"This is not the time to pretend to be a gentleman. I've seen you stare at my tits and my lips and everything else, and you've never acted coy or ashamed. I need to feel something that isn't sadness right now, and I need you to be yourself. I need you to want me, and to take me. Right now. I don't need a nice guy tonight. I need you."

I'm sure there was an insult in there somewhere, but I had spent the last drop of blood in my head when I pulled away, and I couldn't care less.

I pushed forward and took her in my arms again. Her mouth opened eagerly for mine and I kissed her and laid her back against the hard wood of the balcony floor. Her hands danced at my zipper as I yanked my tank top off and tossed it through the open door of my apartment. I kicked my pants off as she removed her shirt to reveal a white, patterned Victoria's Secret bra underneath. Her stomach was smooth and she had a smattering of freckles that I kissed as I unclasped the bra. Then I tugged down her skirt and underwear in one try.

Panting and flushed in the cool night air I took a second to appreciate her body as I ran my fingers down her side and over her hip. She had wide, pink nipples that were reacting perfectly to the cool of the air and the warmth of my touch. Everything beneath her skirt felt as smooth as her stomach, and the tattoo on her leg turned out to be a dragon, whose head ended just below her waist. I smiled when I noticed that she was giving me the once over as well.

She tugged me forward and I ran my finger between her lower lips, which were soft and wet, as I kissed her again. She moaned once more and spread her legs so that I could slide between them. After only a moment of searching we both gasped with pleasure as I found my way home. I slid myself into her warmth slowly, deeper and deeper until she bit my shoulder to keep from yelling out.

We made love, and then we screwed. Over and over. She bit and scratched and moaned, while I kissed and pressed and rolled her over, time and again. We kept it up until we both passed out. The rain died away and the morning sky began to break blue.

When I woke up, I was alone, and morning had come and gone. I sat up, not sure what to make of the previous night, not sure if I would ever be able to look Rachel in the eyes again. Then I saw them. Tucked under the nearly empty bottle of Jameson, on the floor in the corner of the balcony, laid a half-folded pair of light blue cotton panties.

What a great way to start the day.

12 MEAT AND GREET

"Denise Beckham's mother carpet bombed my office with lawyers this morning," ranted David through my earpiece as I cruised west on I-80, toward Sparks. "She just stood there screaming, and some fat bastard ambulance chaser was stacking petitions on my desk, talking about the sanctity of religion and how I was violating Denise's right to have her body untouched after death."

"Can't say I'm sorry I missed that one. The mom is pissed because you guys did an autopsy?"

"It's all bullshit. This case is getting TV coverage all over the goddamn country, and her attorneys are hoping to get a big fat payday, courtesy of the county."

"What are you gonna do?" I asked as I exited the highway and headed north toward a maze of subdivisions born in the last housing boom.

"I have to give up the body. The geeks said they got everything they're gonna get, and if I wind up kicking the shit out of one of her people, we're definitely going to get sued."

I parked in Mr. Williamson's driveway, and shut off the Jeep. It was a single-story house, with a small front lawn and a few trees. "Get through the day. We can blow off some steam tonight."

"Good plan. What are you up to?" My lunch date peeked his head through the curtains of the picture window at the front of the house. I gave him a wave. "Just got to Mr. Williamson's place, one of the teachers from the high school. He might know something about the girls that we haven't heard yet."

"Does he think you're a cop? He better not."

"No, I didn't say I was a cop."

"Why are you at his house then?"

"He told me he'd be okay with answering a couple of questions. He seemed kind of weird, but I'm pretty sure it's only because he was hitting on me."

"Okay sweetheart, remember to use protection."

"Whatever. Free lunch is free lunch."

David hung up and I threw my earpiece into the glove compartment. My Makarov rested in there too, but I didn't think a squirrely school teacher would welcome a gun in his house. I checked my tie in the rearview, straightened my jacket, and got out. By the time I reached the porch, Mr. Williamson stood out front, holding the door open for me.

"So glad you could make it," he smiled and invited me in.

"Sorry about making you wait, I had to finish up a business call."

"No problem at all, I was just putting the finishing touches on lunch anyhow."

As he led me through a modestly decorated living room, the tell-tale scents of grilled meat hit me and I realized that I hadn't eaten anything that morning. "It smells delicious."

"Thank you," he replied as he pointed me to a seat at a built-in dinner table. "I don't mean to brag, but I'm kind of an artist when it comes to preparing meat. I think you'll like it. Can I get you a drink?"

I almost begged off, thought of asking for a glass of water. Then I saw the huge glass liquor cabinet sitting next to the fridge. Johnnie Walker, authentic tequila, old single malts with no labels, and a variety of other delicious beverages were on display. "Sure, whatever you're having is fine."

He poured us drinks and brought out plates full of food. Before long I was halfway through the most delicious pork steak I had ever eaten. "This is amazing," I mumbled between bites. It tasted so good I couldn't even be irked as he chewed with his mouth open. Maybe a little irked.

"I'm glad you like it. Now, you had questions about Denise?"

Oh yeah. I took one last bite and did my best to savor it before putting down my knife and fork. "Right. Anything you could tell me about Denise and her friend, Jennifer..." I looked at the Scotch sitting in front of me, only halfway gone, but I felt properly tipsy. I wondered if I could find a way to get him to gift me the bottle. "Jennifer's mom hired me to look into her disappearance."

"Oh, alright." He smiled and refilled my glass. "Well, as I said before, Denise was great. A real treat. Jennifer as well. She's incredibly tender, wouldn't you say?"

"What? Oh, I didn't know her. Her mom, though... Wow." I couldn't focus. The room started twisting and I had a feeling like I was falling in the pit of my stomach.

"I'm sure she's too old for my tastes, Mr. English. They tend to get stringy after adolescence."

"What?" Somewhere in the back of my mind a tiny voice screamed at me to straighten the fuck up. The same voice I'd heard every time I got pulled over after a bender, back before I decided that paying for a taxi costed a lot less than going to jail, or worse. I shook my head to clear the cobwebs. "What do you mean, '*stringy*?'"

"I think you know exactly what I mean."

I did. Fuck. For the first time, I noticed that his glass hadn't been touched, even though he'd refilled mine once. Or twice? This was not good. The photos of Denise's mangled body invaded my mind. This guy had done that to Denise, and might be doing it to Jennifer.

I wanted to jump up and fight, pin the fucker to the wall. I didn't know if I could. My arms felt like lead and each moment that passed made it harder to keep my head up. My ex-wife roofied me once because she was pissed off about something stupid I'd done or said. This felt worse, and I couldn't imagine waking up to awesome, angry morning sex this time.

"It's you," I slurred. "You... You're a... Fuck... Sick fuck... You."

"Oh, I don't know about that, Mr. English. You seemed to enjoy the meal nearly as much as I did. So, if I'm a 'sick fuck,' what does that make you?"

The pork. Oh god.

My body moved faster than my mind. Before he had a chance to react, I lunged across that table and wrapped my hands around his throat. "YOU FUCK! SICK FUCKING COCKSUCKER!" I caught him off-guard and his face turned red as he fought to gasp for air. He flopped and jerked, knocking things from the table left and right as he tried to get out of my grip. Even drugged, I was stronger than him. I could only hope that he would suffocate before I passed out. I held tight until I saw his eyes roll back into his head. His legs gave out beneath him, and I couldn't hold on any longer. His body hit the floor with a soft *thump*.

I stumbled around the table, leaning heavily on the sturdy wood surface to keep myself upright. He was down, unconscious, at least for the moment. I slapped myself. Again, hard. My legs were shaking and my eyes didn't want to stay open, but somewhere deep inside my brain continued firing on at least one or two cylinders.

I fumbled around in my pocket with my free hand until I found my phone. I stared at the screen until the slider bar finally came into focus. It still took me three tries to get the damn thing to work. David was the last person I talked to, I wouldn't even have to dial a number. Thank Christ.

Green phone button once. Green phone button twice. I put it to my ear. It rang at least four thousand times before he answered, "I'm still at work dammit. Is your date over?"

Come on, mouth, do something!
"It's... Teacher." The room around me started to look like a fucking nightmare. Everything wagged

back and forth and I'm pretty sure David licked my face through the phone.

"What? Are you drunk?"

"No. Drugs."

"Drugs? What the fuck are you talking about?"

"Teacher. Druuuuhhhgs." Come on, I'm speaking clear as day here, David.

"Oh shit, did he try to roofie you?" he laughed.

Come on, Gavin, focus. I picked up my fork from the table and jammed it as hard as I could into my thigh. It helped.

I screamed.

David yelled, "What the hell?!"

"TEACHER! CANNIBAL! DRUGGED ME! HURRY!" I replied sensibly before dropping the phone and yanking the fork out of my leg.

I didn't bleed. At least, I didn't bleed blood. Instead, tiny kittens started oozing their way out of the prong holes on my leg. They were terrifying and cute, but I had work to do.

If this guy was the killer, then Jennifer might be in the house. I had to look. I hefted myself away from the table and stumbled into the living room. I fell twice while swatting at the giant wasps that were trying to get to my blood kittens. Stupid wasps.

There were three doors. One of those doors probably led to Jennifer. The other two were sure to have bears behind them. I picked the one in the middle because I knew I had no time to waste. I gripped the doorknob as tightly as I could and readied to defend myself.

I yanked it open. No bears. "Ha!"

There were stairs, though. About a million of them. I took the first step down, and then the staircase flipped on me. I felt like I was in a dryer during the spin cycle. Over and over the stairs rolled, taking me with them. Luckily, when they stopped spinning, I hit the bottom.

Then the lights went out.***

Robert Williamson was twenty-six when he returned to Salt Lake City from his mission trip to Sierra Leone. Three months after he and his group were kidnapped by insurgents, he alone survived to be rescued by the U.N. peacekeeping force. After going on record about the atrocities he had witnessed, which included rape, torture, and cannibalism, to name a few, he was admitted to a makeshift medical facility. It had been set up in the ruins of a home in the jungle of Western Africa.

Without the tools or personnel necessary to perform skin grafts, they bandaged Robert up and gave him a few days to stabilize before he flew back to the United States. Once in a proper hospital, Robert insisted that he be allowed to remain awake, while the doctors surgically reopened each of the wounds on his legs. With a minimum amount of anesthetic, he watched as metal plates were used to repair the damage that blades and teeth and fire had done to the bones of his leg. Along the edges of his wounds, doctors had to cut away healthy and infected skin alike, to give the skin grafts something to attach to.

He relished the three months he spent healing in that hospital. Medical staff were open about the procedures they used to put his leg back together, as well as the types and doses of pain killers and antibiotics that were needed to keep him comfortable, but still able to function. He asked new questions daily, not only about his body, but about others he saw come in and out. He listened and learned, all the while remembering that first taste of human flesh he had received, while still locked in a cage.

"You wan' stay alive, whito?"

"Yes. Please, I'm starving."

The revolutionary couldn't have been more than 12 years old, but when he smiled, Robert saw that his teeth were rotting out of his head. "Then you eat this, whito. Is all we got to give you."

He cringed and gagged at the *thought*, but the barely cooked flesh exploded in a burst of flavor in his mouth. Tender. Delicious. He asked for more.

Back in the states, he was released from the hospital and the Church paid for him to get into an apartment. Soon after, he enrolled in classes at a community college, and got started on his education degree.

Another ninety days went by before he could no longer ignore the hunger.

"Hey, you need a ride?" Robert asked the young nursing student as he slowed his 4x4 near the curb where she was walking. The snow storm had arrived unexpectedly, and it came in with a vengeance.

"Yes, please!" she said as he opened the passenger side door for her. "It's freezing out here and I didn't even bring a jacket because it was so nice this morning."

He drove back out into the empty street, slowly, to keep from slipping on the snow and ice. He watched from the corner of his eye as she brushed dewy flakes from her hair and wiped the moisture from her face. She had pretty, soft features and couldn't have been more than nineteen years old.

"Where can I take you?"

"It's only up on Redwood Road. Any further than that and I would have to give in and get myself a car," she laughed.

He slammed on the brakes, sending the pickup spinning to the side of the road, and the girl crashing into the dashboard. Once stopped, he leapt across bench seat and wrapped his forearm under girl's chin, squeezing her windpipe closed. She kicked and grunted and scratched at his arms, but within seconds she fell limp.

He reached into his glove compartment and grabbed the bottle of Percocet he had saved from his pain treatment. With shaking hands, he fished out three pills, pinched her nose closed, and forced the pills down her throat. Then he got back on the road.

Robert navigated his car east, through the storm. He drove for nearly two hours, out onto a remote salt flat, far outside the city. There was no traffic, no road crews, nothing for forty miles. He shut the pickup off, making sure to remove the keys so the battery wouldn't lose charge. Then he got out, opened the door to the camper shell, and yanked the nursing student from the cab of the truck. She was heavier than he expected, but he didn't have much trouble getting her to the back. Once her body was safely out of the weather, he climbed in behind her, and closed the camper door.

For the next two and a half hours, Robert tested the limits of the human body. With a butcher's knife and a pair of pliers, he ripped through the nursing student's arms and legs. He cut around the skin on her kneecap, and then ripped it off with his teeth. He gorged himself on her flesh until he threw up, and then started eating again. Each new slice tasted different, the heel of her foot, the muscle of her upper thigh, a hunk of breast meat, her cheek. When she finally died, he laid in the ocean of blood that had pooled in the bed of his truck and masturbated.

Once finished, he bagged up their clothes and tossed them into the cab. Then, he detached the camper shell and shoved it off into the snow that covered the salt flat. Using the falling snow and a broom, he swept the nursing student's body, the blood, and most of the mess out of the truck bed.

He made it home before daylight and cleaned the remaining mess with bleach and a mop. When he woke up the next morning, his pickup was covered in white powder again. Before the snow around Salt Lake City could melt, Robert packed everything he owned and moved to Portland.

These were the memories that haunted his dreams. As the taste of the blood, and the rush of his first time started to fade, he knew he was waking up.

13 SMALL MIRACLES

His eyes opened, but nothing he saw made sense. Directly above him he could see wood paneling and his legs were tangled in a chair. His head throbbed and there was a dull ache that went from his Adam's apple to the top of his sternum. He turned his head slowly to take in his surroundings. He saw his refrigerator, his linoleum covered floor on which he lay, and the chair that his feet were tangled up in belonged to him as well. Home.

With one question answered, the rest came back to him in a rush. He stopped struggling and slid his feet away from the chair. He had no idea how long he had been out, but he could hear someone moving around in the other room. For a moment, he worried that it may be the police, but he heard mumbling and grunting and then whoever it was yelled and fell to the floor. It had to be English, and from the sound of it, the drugs were working hard. He rolled over and climbed to his feet without making a sound. The private detective had found his feet again in the living room, and he flailed and grunted his way over and around furniture. For a brief second, Williamson worried about all the cleaning he would have to do once the drugs finally put the man under.

Pressed to the wall, he slithered his way down the short hallway until he came to the edge of the living room. Sure enough, English stood there, head lolling on his shoulders and legs threatening to give out as he stared at the door that led down to the basement.

A second of panic as he pictured the man finding Jennifer, tied to the bed with nearly twenty ounces of flesh stripped from her legs. But he knew that the drugs were still there, pumping heavier through the man's blood stream every second. And there was another bed.

Careful to avoid the toppled end tables, lamps, and other furnishings littering the floor, Williamson crept through the room until he was only a foot away from the private detective. Anticipation surged throughout his body as English yanked the door open and then shook his fist threateningly into the darkness. "Ha!" he yelled out, oblivious to the predator in the room with him.

Williamson inched closer as the man lifted his foot slowly, apparently planning to go down the staircase. Then he shoved him, as hard as could, and looked on gleefully as English tumbled down the steps and slammed hard into the door at the bottom.

In the sliver of pale light streaming down from the living room, he saw that the man's eyes were still open. Frustrated and disappointed, Williamson slammed the door shut and left the private detective in the darkness.***

The light bulb hanging between the beds kept Jennifer from being able to get any real sleep. It added to the constant pain in her legs. Little things like an itch on her nose or a fly landing on her face became endless tortures as she lay, unable to move, strapped to the bed. On her first day, he confided to her that the room was soundproof, and no one would ever hear her cries. So, in the hours while she occupied the room alone, she would find solace in crying or screaming or cursing the man who put her there.

Now though, she wondered about the person who he had talked about. Would it be someone that she knew? Another student? Or would it be someone like him, another person to hurt her and haunt her dreams? Was there any chance in the world that it would be someone who might be able to help her?

She didn't dare to think of that.

She only knew for sure that it was a man, or possibly a boy. Williamson had said that he had invited "him" over, before he started cutting on her good leg. Thinking about it made the throbbing more pronounced. She thought about the new person instead.

Could having someone else down in the basement with her make things easier? Maybe talking, getting shit out of her head, would help her forget about the pain. Or, would things be darker? She didn't want to imagine Williamson cutting on someone else, or even worse, having to eat another person's flesh.

A thump on the door. He was coming in.

Her pulse raced and it became harder to breathe as a familiar wave of panic took over.***

"Hell no."

Captain Meadows sat behind his desk with a sour look on his face. It was the same look David saw every time he mentioned anal sex to his ex-girlfriend. The look said that there would be no discussion.

"Captain, I get that you don't trust Gavin. Hell, I don't trust him half the time either. But this is important."

"Goddammit, Reeves. You can't come in here and tell me that Gavin Fucking English called you up, pissed out of his gourd, and had something important to say. I'm not giving that sack of crap a handful of my guys to lead around on a wild goose chase."

David bit back an angry reply. Getting into trouble just then wouldn't help anyone. "Well do I have permission to check it out at least?"

"I don't care what you do. But if a call goes out anywhere near you, you better forget your drinking buddy and get your ass on scene. Got that?"

"Got it."

He ducked out of the big man's office and made his way across the department floor, doing his best not to make eye contact with anyone. If Gavin was screwing around, he wanted as few people as possible to know that he'd been truly worried.

Once out of the building, he rushed to his Crown Victoria and found the number to the school on his phone. It rang three times.

"Principal's office," answered the old woman, who he remembered from his last visit to the school.

"Hello, this is Lieutenant Reeves. I had a meeting with Mr. Rawlings yesterday."

"Oh, yes. Hello, Officer Reeves. How can I help you? I'm afraid Mr. Rawlings is visiting a class right now."

"That's fine. I just needed to get an address for one of your teachers there. I think it was a Mr. Williams."

"I'm sorry, sir, we don't have a Mr. Williams here."

"I might have the wrong name. Is one of your teachers absent today?"

"Oh! Mr. Williamson, yes. He's out today, is that who you meant?"

"Yes, ma'am." David started the car and waited for the GPS to power up. "What address do you have for Mr. Williamson?"

The old woman rambled off an address and David entered it into his navigation system.

"May I ask what it is you want with Mr. Williamson?"

"We just have a few questions to ask him. Thank you," he replied and then hung up. He tried Gavin's phone one more time.

Straight to voicemail.***

I don't know if I got an adrenaline kickstart from falling down the stairs or from the
ribs that were definitely broken, but right after everything went dark, the druggy fog faded. This was good because the shitty situation I now found myself

in had every intention of getting worse real quick, and I needed my head on straight. It was bad, though, because I had stabbed myself in the leg with a dirty fork and then went head over heels a few times down a concrete staircase.

Every-single-damn-thing hurt, from a gash in my scalp that trickled blood into my eye, to my ribs, which were trying to escape from my body, down to my ankle that didn't seem to fit within the confines of my sock. I took a few breaths, savoring the pain as it cleaned out the cobwebs. Things did not look good for me and Jennifer.

I left my gun in the Jeep, which might as well have been a bank vault for all the good it would do me now. Williamson was nuttier than squirrel shit, had a taste for long pork, and Jennifer and I were in his creepy, super-villain lair. To top it all off, if it turned out I picked the wrong door, then I wound up busted to pieces at the bottom of dark staircase, with no idea where he had her tucked away, or how I could get to her. Oh well, no time to wallow in self-pity.

I found my feet, and used the wall to steady myself as I tried to get on top of them. It hurt, but I'd been banged up and squiffy plenty of times before. It felt a bit like riding a bike. It took a minute to get my bearings with the lights out, but before long I found the big pull handle on the door. It reminded me of the huge steel doors they use on meat lockers; this thought did not bring me any comfort. I guessed I had as much chance of finding a fridge full of body parts, as I did of finding Jennifer.

And then there was light.

It burned my eyes and raked through my skull like a fork on a chalk board. I flinched and blinked a thousand times. Eventually my brain began to build a picture of the room behind the big door. I was in the right place. A rectangular room decorated in all concrete and metal, with a naked bulb dangling between two hospital beds. The room reeked of blood and chemicals and urine. The far bed had someone in it, unmoving and naked except for strips of bloody cotton that were being used to bandage her legs. I shut the door behind me.

"Jennifer?" I didn't whisper, but my voice sounded low compared the beating of my heart. What if I had come too late? I took a step forward and my shoe on the concrete sounded like a hammer in the dull silence of the room. She flinched at the sound. Thank god.

"Jennifer, it's alright." I crossed the room, favoring my swollen ankle. "It's alright. He's not here."

She started crying, hard and fast and wet. When I got to the side of the bed, I started unlashing one of the straps pinning her down, the one which held her head first. Her eyes were closed but the tears kept coming, washing away the stains of so many tears that had come before.

When the strap came undone, she moved her head slowly, testing the freedom. I moved on to the next strap without speaking. Then the next, and the next, until there were none left to keep her down. She barely moved, and her eyes were still locked shut.

I took off my jacket; it glistened with blood, but it was large enough that she could cover most of her body with it. "Here, Jennifer. Put this on."

She opened her eyes finally, and I tried to
help her sit up. She flinched and bit down on her lip,
but once she stabilized she wrapped the coat around
herself.

"Are you a cop?" Her whole body shook like she
was freezing, and her voice shook right along with it.

"Not exactly. Your mom hired me to help find
you. They're on the way, though." I couldn't be sure
if they were or not. I knew I had called David, but I
had no idea if he got the message out of my drugged
ranting.

She wiped her face clean with the sleeve of my
jacket. "He killed Denise. It's Mr. Williamson. He
killed her."

"I know. Don't worry about that right
now, hun."

She nodded, fresh tears broke the
dam. Somehow, my cigarettes and lighter were still in
my breast pocket. A minor miracle. I lit up, offered
one to the girl. She accepted. I lit one for her.

"I'm only seventeen," she said after her first
drag.

"Once we get out of here, a fine for giving a
minor a smoke will feel like a medal of honor."

She laughed. Another miracle.

14 ONE SHOT

He paced the length of the kitchen and dining room, grinding his teeth and rubbing his knuckles over and over. His mind jumped from thoughts of running, disappearing into the world, to thoughts of the heaven that awaited if he could get that damned detective under his knife. As he stepped past the table one more time, he picked up the bottle that had failed him. The GHB had worked, of that he had no doubt. And yet, English was still awake.

He imagined being the type of person who would scream out in his anger, throw the bottle and watch as it exploded into a satisfying mess of booze and shards of glass. That kind of anger was wasteful and useless to a man like Williamson, who planned and adapted for every situation. Instead, he placed the bottle back in his liquor cabinet, and locked it.

No, rage would exacerbate this situation. He walked to the living room and began cleaning up the day's mess. An end table laid overturned on its side. He lifted it back to its place, picked up the papers and notebooks that had fallen from its drawers, and replaced the lamp that had gone down with it. Thankfully, nothing was broken. He put couch cushions back in their proper place, straightened his diploma and degree certificates, which had been knocked askew, and rehung his winter coat, which had fallen from its place on the coat rack.

Then, he found the cell phone. English's cell phone. It had hit the floor hard enough to crack the screen and knock the battery loose, but that didn't mean he hadn't used it. He picked up the pieces, slid the battery back into place, and put it back together. It wouldn't turn on. For several minutes, he stood and stared as he tried to figure out what it could mean. What were the chances that English could use the phone in his drug addled state? Who might he have called? Were the police on their way?

Fight or Flight.

Nearly ten minutes had gone by since he shoved English down the stairs. If he had managed to call the police, they were well on their way. Getting away without being noticed would be almost impossible, if they were. With a locked door and several warnings to get through before they could come in, though, he still had plenty of time to enjoy himself in the basement. A last meal, and then he could make himself a cocktail of drugs that would send him off nicely. No prison.

And, if they were not on their way, then there was no reason to hurry. He could put the girl down, enjoy a hearty slice of English, and then saunter out of town before anyone knew what had happened.

Either way, the party would start in the basement.***

"What's your name?" she asked.

"Gavin."

"He's still up there, isn't he?"

"What?" I was thinking of ways to get to my gun, or any weapon that could help us get out of there, and her question caught me off guard.

"Mr. Williamson is still up there. That's why we're not leaving, isn't it?"

"Yeah." I didn't have any comfort to give her; I wasn't going to lie. "I think he meant to put me in the other bed but the drugs didn't leave me as far under as he thought they would."

"Oh. What are you going to do?"

Good question. I had no idea. "We'll just wait it out down here."

"Do you have a gun?"

"It's in my car."

"Oh." I could hear hopelessness creeping into her voice. "He has knives and stuff down here." She pointed to the counter with the big, metal sink. "Maybe there's something you could use."

Sure enough, when I looked in the sink I found a plethora of surgical tools and kitchen knives, all soaking in an acetone bath. There were scalpels and hypodermic needles, and a few other things I recognized. There were also huge, jagged saw blades and other, more insidious items that looked like holdovers from medieval torture rooms.

I lifted out two of the bigger kitchen knives, and set one next to Jennifer in the bed. She didn't say anything, but I could see she didn't like having it there. Her eyes shifted nervously from the blade to the door, and back again.

"It's for protection, Jennifer," I said, trying to keep her calm. "I don't think you'll even have to touch it, but it's better to be safe than sorry."

"Oh," she replied.

The pain from my ribs grew with every breath I took, and I knew that it would get to be overwhelming before long. "What does he use the needles for?"

"He gave me pain killers with a needle the first time." She stared down at her legs for the first time and her eyes started to water heavily again. "He didn't use it on my right leg."

Sadistic son of a bitch. I wished I could have squeezed harder when I had my hands around his throat. This girl would never feel safe with this guy alive, even if he was behind bars.

"Do you know where the drugs are, where he keeps them?"

She looked up at me with those big sad eyes. "Maybe by the sink, I'm not sure. I heard him messing around over in that cabinet too, but I could never see what he was doing." After fishing around the counter and sink for a minute, I crossed the room and opened the metal cabinet. Hanging there were blood stained smocks, clean plastic aprons, a couple pairs of worker's coveralls, and a box of dishwasher's gloves on the floor. Above the hanging rack was a shelf, the shelf where I found our salvation.

Vials of oxycodone, morphine, oxycontin, and several other drugs whose names I couldn't pronounce lined the shelf, along with dozens of brand new hypodermic needles. I grabbed a vial of the oxycodone, because I didn't remember hearing as many horror stories about it as I had with the others, and two of the syringes, still cozy in their plastic wrappers." What are you doing?" Jennifer asked with an edge of panic to her voice.

I limped back to the counter with the sink and set everything down. "When I fell down those stairs, I broke a couple ribs. If I don't do something about it quick, I might pass out from the pain. That wouldn't be good for either of us."

"Okay, but I don't want any shots," her voice trembled again.

I tore one of the needles from its packaging, removed the plastic lid, and jammed the thing through the rubber stopper on the medicine's jar. "Listen, Jennifer. I know it's been a while since you've had anything for the pain, and it's got to be getting bad."

"I don't care. Please. I don't want any more needles. I'll be fine."

I only filled the syringe about a quarter of the way. I'm not a doctor, and although I wanted to relieve the pain, I didn't want to overdo it. I tapped the thing like I had seen on the tube a million times, and pressed the plunger until I was sure there were no bubbles.

"I don't suppose you wanna play nurse for a second?" I asked, knowing the answer.

She shook her head. Oh well.

I unbuttoned my shirt and lifted the bottom of my tank top. It was not pretty. Angry purple and yellow-green bruises painted my ribcage, from my nipple to my navel. I took a deep breath to steady my hand and pressed the cold needle right to the center of the darkest bruise I could see. I pushed down until it broke through the skin.

It hurt as badly as you might think. I bit my lip until I could taste blood and depressed the plunger. The clear liquid felt like ice as it flowed into the muscles along my ribs. I let go of the breath I'd been holding, and the magic of the dope became instantly clear. I could breathe, and move, without feeling woozy. Goddamn, that was nice.

I dropped my tank top, and buttoned my shirt back up. "That's better," I said, giving Jennifer a smile. She didn't return it. I ripped open the other syringe.

"I said I don't want any. Please."

"It's not for you, Jenny," I replied as I stabbed the needle into the vial and pulled up another half syringe full of oxycodone. "I'm putting this one up for later," I gave her wink and put the plastic cap back onto the needle. I set the syringe on the counter. It all looked so medical, I couldn't imagine being in that room for as long as Jennifer had, without going crazy.

"No... no... no..." she stuttered behind me.

"I said it's not for you..." I turned around and saw what set her off. Williamson was standing in the doorway.

15 BLOOD AND STARS

David parked in the driveway, behind the red Jeep he had seen so many times before. He knew he'd found the right place, but still had no real idea about why he had come. He climbed out of the Crown Vic, checked to make sure the button on his holster was unlocked, and shut the door as he walked toward the house.

It seemed cozy enough, but he proceeded with the caution, which came from nine years on the force. The door was closed, but the curtains in the picture window were parted. As he got closer, he looked in. He couldn't see any sign of a struggle. The furniture seemed to all be in place, and he heard no sounds coming from inside.

He stepped up onto the porch and knocked three times, with his free hand resting on the pistol at his hip.***

He didn't move. He stood there staring at me with a smile that made my skin crawl. I took three steps to Jennifer's bed and slid in front of her. "The cops are on their way, Williamson. Walk out now and you might be able to get away."

He stepped into the room and shut the door behind him. The door creaked. Had it creaked when he came in? How did I not notice?

He rolled the locking bar into place. "Why would I want to leave?" The awful smile melted away as he pulled the biggest Ginsu I'd ever seen from the back of his pants. "I haven't had dinner yet."

Jennifer snatched up the blade she had been so frightened of not long ago, and held it out with both hands. I kept my knife low, still hoping to talk him out of whatever he had planned.

"It's not going to happen. Walk away, let Jennifer go, and maybe you get life in prison. Keep it up, and there's only one way out for you."

"You don't understand," he replied taking a step forward. I lifted the blade in my hand a bit higher. "I've already resigned myself to my fate. It's you that doesn't realize there is only one way out of this."

"You're not hurting this girl anymore, Williamson."

I smelled my own sweat and fear, mixed with Jennifer's. Our host acted calm and collected, despite the situation. This did not reassure me. I still wasn't one hundred percent, and I had no idea if this guy had any combat training or if he was a paperback psycho, who liked to pick on people smaller than him. Judging by the hollow look in his eyes, I was about to find out.

He didn't reply. Jennifer's ragged breathing filled the room, and I could feel her body tremble behind me. Probably good that she hadn't accepted any pain killers after all.

I rolled the knife handle around in my hand, getting a feel for it as I sized up the maniac across from me. He had to be a full six feet tall, and weighed around a buck-ninety. Not out of shape, but not athletic either. His eyes were blank and his stare gave nothing away. Nothing that would help anyway.

His leg twitched, and his body went rigid. His knuckles bleached white around the handle of the blade and he flicked his wrist once. Twice. Then he rushed forward.

I twisted right, with his momentum, and pushed him away from Jennifer's bed with my empty hand. He snarled as he swung out with that vicious blade, barely missing Jennifer. She screamed and rolled away, nearly falling from the bed.

With his attention turned to her for the second, I yanked his shoulder back hard and slid my knife between his ribs and his left arm. It only made light contact, but he turned his rage back on me. He escaped my one-handed grip and took a clumsy step back. Williamson bared his teeth like a dog, spittle trailing from both corners of his mouth.

He lunged again. This time I couldn't turn the attack and I took the full weight of his shoulder in my aching ribcage. I saw stars. Stars like you see when you go camping with your old man. I knew I couldn't hang onto the blade and keep from going unconscious at the same time. My hand loosened, and somewhere at the end of the starry tunnel, I heard my knife hit the floor. But I was still awake.

The force of his tackle took us to the far wall. We hit hard, back first, then my head. Then I felt him run that cold steel up the back of my right thigh. The stars faded as the new wound blazed to life. I finally reacted.

His head was low. I swung deep with my right fist and caught him in the sternum. He stepped back and straightened up enough that my left landed square on his chin. He stumbled away from me. His gaze unfocused, but he still had an iron grip on the handle of that Ginsu.

I swung again and came up short of his jaw, but it made him take another step back toward the sink. With both fists up, I bobbed off the wall, doing my best to ignore the screaming pain rolling through my body. A jab with my left barely connected, I missed with my right. I had him on the ropes.

My mistake was not keeping my attention on his eyes. They weren't glazed anymore. I threw another jab with my left, but this time when he leaned back, he lashed out with that goddamn knife. It went deep into my forearm, hit the bone hard enough that I almost went under again. This time, I jumped back.

My right pant leg and shoe were cold and soaked with blood already, and now my arm was gushing. My fingers went numb right away, and I knew that with the blood loss, I wouldn't be on my feet for long.

He smiled at me again. The swollen, purple welt across his jaw did not make his look any more appetizing. Behind him, I could see Jennifer watching us, still clutching the knife with a crazed and terrified look in her eyes. I couldn't leave her alone with him again.***

David tried Gavin's number one last time. Straight to voicemail. He hammered his knuckles on the whitewashed door for the umpteenth time. No response. No sound at all from inside. Gavin's Jeep still sat there in the driveway; someone should be able to hear him knocking or ringing the doorbell. Something was wrong.

He weighed the pros and cons of kicking his way in. If Gavin was fine, or drunk, or high, then it would be his ass for going into a home without probable cause. He couldn't hear any screaming; there were no bodies or drugs or blood anywhere to be seen. Worst of all, his intel relied on the one man he knew the Captain didn't trust.

But, if there was something wrong and he walked away... If Gavin was in there with the person who had killed Denise Beckham, or if the other missing girl was in there and still alive...

David stepped back and took a deep breath. "IT'S THE POLICE! WE'RE COMING IN!" he shouted before taking his boot to the door. Once. Twice. Three times before it gave way.

"POLICE!" he barked again as he made his way inside.

16 THE STARS AND THE DARKNESS

"You're feeling it, Mr. English. Soon, your body will give out for lack of blood. All I have to do is wait."

He wasn't wrong. I was woozy, and I had a chill I knew had nothing to do with the temperature. I had to do something, and I had to do it soon. I couldn't give him the chance to wait me out.

I took my turn to rush in. I was hurt and angry and quite frankly, scared shitless. I moved as fast as my legs would carry me, and clearly he hadn't expected me to do something that reckless in my condition. His eyes went wide and he started to dodge a second too late. I crashed into him with my full weight and pinned him against the counter so that his back twisted and bent the wrong way.

I slugged him as hard as I could with my left to his gut, and then threw an elbow that landed right in his throat. He gagged and screamed and forced me back a step. Williamson swung the Ginsu out, wide, in an arc that nearly got my good arm. Again and again he swung the blade, gripping his throat with his free hand and clearly having a hard time catching a breath.

I hopped back and felt my right leg wobble beneath me. The stars were coming back and my stomach lurched several times, threatening to eject all of its contents. I watched Williamson struggle and I barely dodged the blade as it whipped out at me, back and forth. I knew it would be risking more blood, but I could feel unconsciousness nipping at my heels. I moved in again.

His arm went out, away from his body. I tightened up and dug myself right into his chest with my shoulder. Something cracked under my weight and his gasp of air shot spit out across my neck. He rolled me left and my ribs slammed into the counter as he shoved and scratched at my face. He pressed and I felt myself give in to his strength as he leaned me backwards, over the sink.

He raised the blade over both our heads and I raised my bad arm defensively, hoping that he couldn't make it hurt any worse. When his swing came down, though, it was weak, and the knife glanced off my arm without doing any real damage. Each breath he took shuddered as bad as my own, and his eyes were glossing over more with each passing moment.

He swung at me once more and I twisted to my left, again his blow fell on my useless appendage. His attack had nothing behind it but his body weight pushed me back, and my good arm slid along the counter until my elbow hung uselessly over the sink. As I fought to lift myself out of my contorted position, my fingers found the syringe I had placed there minutes ago.

At first I thought of using it on myself. My second thought was more helpful.

As he raised up to swing the blade again, I locked the syringe in my grip and swept it upward. With a soft crunching sound more satisfying than sex, the needle landed home in the soft skin between his Adam's apple and his jaw.

"*GnnnaKKKKsssss,*" was all he said as I shoved the plunger home, forcing the oxycodone out through the needle's head.

I heard the Ginsu hit the counter next to me, then the ground. Williamson leaned further onto me, hissing and gurgling as his eyes rolled into the back of his head. I let go of the empty syringe and left it dangling from his pasty flesh. Then his knees buckled and he hit the floor. I almost followed him down, but I still had one good arm holding me up on the counter.

Jennifer screamed and fell off the bed, still gripping that knife. She landed with a dull thud and a grunt.

"I'm okay!"

She screamed again as something started pounding on the door to the room. I didn't hear voices or anything from outside, but the heavy steel door kept juttering and shaking. Someone was trying to get inside.

"Coming," I announced, donning my best Ward Cleaver voice.

It may have taken me an hour to get there, but after much stumbling and limping and cussing, and even more bleeding, I made it to the door. The lock slid up easily, and as it came open I saw the prettiest face I had ever seen. It was David, and he caught me just as my legs, and the rest of my body, finally gave up.

"Gavin! Oh shit," he said as he set me on the floor. He was gentle, I'll give him that. He pulled out his cell phone and dialed a number, "This is Lieutenant Reeves, I need an ambulance and a couple of black and whites at one-three-nine-nine Elm St." He listened, then, "Yes. Hurry."

"It's gotta be nice to be the boss," I said as he shoved the phone back in his pocket.

He found his gun with his free hand and gave the room a cursory glance. I had left Jennifer on the floor, between the beds, and Williamson was on the far side of the room. David didn't see either of them. "This fucking place stinks. What happened to you? Are you alone in here? Have you seen the other girl?" he rattled off questions as he tried to make sense of the scene.

"YOU MOTHER FUCKER!" Jennifer screamed from the other side of the room. "I FUCKING HATE YOU!" A wet thud echoed, followed by another, and then the sound of something splattering against the wall. "BASTARD! FUCKING BASTARD! I HATE YOU!"

"Shit!" David rushed across the room. I couldn't see anything. "Jennifer? Jennifer, listen to me. My name is Lieutenant David Reeves, I'm here to help. I need you to put the knife down."

"NO!" she yelled again. Another wet thump. More splattering sounds.

"Jennifer," said David. Then I heard a struggle, kicking and grunting and Jennifer cursing, until finally I saw that David had his arms around her waist as he dragged her back toward me. She continued kicking and fighting, but she stopped screaming, and no longer had the knife in her hand. She was covered in fresh blood, though, and her sobs wracked her body from head to toe.

"It's okay, Jenny," I said as they got closer, doing my best to reassure the young girl. "It's okay." Then the room faded and the stars and the darkness took over.

17 IN THE HOSPITAL

"Of course, he didn't die. That would have done all of us a favor, and he doesn't do favors."

I have no idea how long I was out, but I knew that if her voice had to be the first thing I heard, the universe must hate me. Her Wal-Mart perfume wafted through the room strong enough to gag a maggot, so I tried to hold my breath. Nothing in this world was going to get me to open my eyes and have her be the first thing I saw after what I had been through.

"That's cold," came a familiar voice from the other side of the room. "You should go. Visit later when Gavin's had time to recuperate." Good old David. He pretends not to like me sometimes, but deep down, I always knew he had my back.

"'Who the hell do you think you are? This is my husband and I will stay in this room until I know that he's alright."

"Yvette, you two have been divorced for a couple of years now. Remember? That's why you're shacked up with another guy. Now you need to go, or I'm going to call a few officers up here to put you in handcuffs."

Come on, David, don't threaten her with a good time. She'll never leave.

"Whatever. I'll come back when you're not here polishing his knob."

"Yvette, please let's just go...?" pleaded Mike from behind them.

Holy shit, that guy was in the room the whole time? I almost blew my cover and started laughing right then.

"Fine, fine," she replied. I listened as she grumbled and stomped her way across the room, then I heard a door open and close.

"Is she gone?" I whispered.

"You dick," answered David. "You could've opened your eyes and told her to go to hell."

"But it was so much better hearing you do it."

We both laughed, but I stopped quickly because the pain in my ribs flared up. It was bearable, but definitely not fun. I looked around as I caught my breath. We were unmistakably in a hospital room, with its generic floral paintings and the smells of piss and bleach. Even so, knowing I had gotten out of that sicko's basement made me feel like I had been sleeping in a generous stripper's cleavage.

"How you doin?" asked David.

"I have no idea. My ribs hurt, but not too bad. Whatever they've got running in that I.V. is nice and warm."

"I think it's Morphine. You got pretty torn up, Gavin."

"Tell me something I don't know."

"Okay. How about good news? The girl's doing well. She's in another room. Her mom hasn't left the hospital since you two got here."

I closed my eyes. She was alright. Maybe I wasn't as useless as Yvette thought after all. "What are they gonna do about her legs?"

"The doc said she'll be like new after a couple of surgeries and a lot of physical therapy."

"Good. Any chance I can smoke in here?"

David laughed.

"What about Williamson?" I asked finally.

"Dead. She stabbed him half a dozen times and he bled out in minutes."

"Good." The door to my room opened and Rachel walked in, legs and all.

"You're awake," she smiled as she approached the hospital bed. "You look good."

"Liar," I laughed. "It's good to see you."

"You too." She leaned over and kissed my forehead. "Jennifer wanted me to thank you. She would come visit, but she's stuck in her own bed still."

"Tell her I'm glad she's okay. How are you?"

David got up from his seat next to the bed, "I'm gonna go get coffee. I'll be back to check in on you in a little while, Gavin."

After he closed the door I turned my attention back to Rachel. She looked away as the tears started building up. "I can't believe this happened. I can't believe that my little girl had to..." She snuffled and plucked a tissue from the box next to my bed. Even through the tears and the exhaustion, she was gorgeous. "It's a lot, you know?"

"Yeah."

"I'm taking her back East. I need to be closer to my family. Jennifer says she wants to go, doesn't want to be in a place where everyone has heard about this. She's afraid people will treat her differently."

Shit. I was hoping she'd be around long enough to divorce me at least. Oh well. "She's right, they probably would."

She straightened up and wiped the last stray tear from her cheek. "There's a good physical therapist, who my dad knows. Jennifer's going to do most of her work there."

I thought of my balcony, and the whiskey, and the light blue panties. "I'm sure it'll be better for both of you to have family around to help you get through it all."

"Yeah, I think so too."

"Yeah."

"Thank you, Gavin." She leaned in again and hugged me, and then handed me an envelope. "I'll never be able to repay you for what you did."

I stuttered, trying to find a response, but before I could say a word she was out the door. I fumbled with the envelope for a second before I got it opened.

I pulled out a photo of Jennifer and Rachel, from before, standing in front of a car. On the back of the photo, "Jenny's first car!" had been scribbled in blue ink. It was a nice picture; they were both smiling like loonies. I hoped they would be able to smile like that again soon.

Behind the picture were five crisp one-hundred-dollar bills. Enough for a few good nights at the bar, to help me forget.

ABOUT THE AUTHOR

Ken Lindsey was born in Salt Lake City, Utah to an outlaw father who read him Sesame Street books at bedtime and let him watch *The Shining* before his fifth birthday, and a blue-collar mother who was likely the hardest working person he has ever met. This is how he wound up spending most of his childhood with his nose in books and a die-hard love of horror movies and great cinema in general. Narnia, the Millennium Falcon, and Elm Street all hold holy and happy places in his adolescent memories.

During high school Ken found his true love in a Journalism class where he wrote opinion pieces, toyed with the idea of being a photo-journalist, and took every chance he got to read and review books that had not already found their way to his bookshelf. Before graduation, he began writing his first manuscript-a vampire story very reminiscent of Anne Rice's *Interview with a Vampire*, which was never (and never will be) published or shared with the public-at-large.

Since graduating Salutatorian of his class, Ken has dabbled in College, tried his hand far too many jobs to name, married, had four beautiful children, divorced, and continued writing. Nowadays he drinks all the coffee, spends as much time as he can with his children, enjoys the Pacific coast whenever he can get to it, and perseveres in his writing in between bouts of vacuuming animal fur from the couch and searching for the best biscuits and gravy in the Pacific Northwest.

To find out more: **KenLindseyBooks.com**

www.ingramcontent.com/pod-product-compliance
Lightning Source LLC
Chambersburg PA
CBHW031152160726
47992CB00006B/2420